HERCULINE

A NOVEL

GRACE BYRON

LONDON NEW YORK TORONTO
AMSTERDAM/ANTWERP NEW DELHI SYDNEY/MELBOURNE

1230 AVENUE OF THE AMERICAS, NEW YORK, NEW YORK 10020

First Saga Press hardcover edition October 2025

Interior design by Lewelin Polanco

Manufactured in the United States of America

10 9 8 7 6 5 4 3 2 1

Library of Congress Cataloging-in-Publication Data has been applied for.

ISBN 978-1-6680-8786-2
ISBN 978-1-6680-8788-6 (ebook)

To Dana, with all my love

My kinky roleplay: I am an honest person. I am not ashamed of myself.

—**LAUREN COOK**

HERCULINE

PART 1

FEMALE SMALL BUSINESS OWNER

I no longer believe in salvation. But for years I tried to escape the magnetic pull of the demonic. I repented for as long as I could, then moved to New York. Unfortunately, I did not arrive in the city alone.

Most days I woke up at three in the morning in a cold sweat, face-to-face with a sleep paralysis demon. Sometimes I would cower in fear. Sometimes I would ask it what Satan thought about #MeToo. The demons never laughed. I'd seen evil spirits since long before I moved to New York, but I had hoped that moving away from Indiana would help. All God's children enter the world innocent, naive, and prone to poor life choices.

One bitter autumn, I woke up to a man in a crooked hat standing in the corner of my room. The wind howled like a banshee against the window.

"Does Satan enforce a dress code?" I asked.

"Sometimes," he said.

He wore a sharp black suit. The closer I looked at his face, the stranger it seemed, warped green clay squelched into a single red orb.

By then I knew I wasn't the only one who experienced such phenomena. I'd read about other people's nightmares: clowns, glazy-eyed twinks, bimbos with fangs, cops, a bunch of pigs in a trench coat.

"You never told me your name," I said. The entity was silent. "Why are you here?"

"I am but one of many."

"I've never met a girl demon," I said. "Are there any?"

He didn't respond, still as a sentinel in the corner. Usually after a few hours the demons just vanished. For a while the impermanence gave me a false sense of security—like maybe it was all a dream. But they always came back, as graceless and stoic as before. The harm they caused had been, so far, purely psychological.

When I was a child, I used to see things during the day. I drew oil crosses on the window. That mostly kept them away, but it also made me nauseous. Like I was wicked myself. As I got older they only ever came to me during those twilight hours when I was half asleep. Plausible deniability.

Since I almost always slept alone, no one ever heard me scream. Not that I screamed a lot. Sometimes the demons were just scarier. Occasionally one of the trans boys I slept with would let me stay over. The demons never came then. They wanted me alone.

"He is coming," the demon said.

"Who?"

He stood wordlessly as I turned over, fed up with the stonewalling.

Eventually, the spirit turned to mist and receded into the wall. I got up and checked my phone to see if Max, my trans boy of the hour, had messaged me. I had his shot day memorized so I could tell when he would be ready for a testosterone-fueled bender. There was nothing.

I didn't have an alarm clock, but I did have a half-empty bag of ketamine, an old mug of coffee, and two stolen vials of perfume. Enough to start my day.

After a bump, I hopped into the shower to try and shake the nightmare from my body. My landlord texted me asking for my rent to be deposited online instead of mailed. He wasn't a very nice man, but then again, God, our heavenly landlord, isn't the nicest man either. I know this because I used to pray the way my mother taught me—begging for rent money. So far I've never received a check.

In the kitchen, my roommate was making herself bacon, eggs, and coffee since she worked from home. We performed our cohabitation pleasantries.

I smiled at her. "Smells good."

"Thank you," she said.

She never offered me any. The bacon smelled kind of burnt anyway. I ran downstairs and went to the bodega where I filled a large coffee and grabbed a banana. A man standing in front of the ice cream section yelled something obscene about cutting me open and feeding me to the pigeons.

"Sounds good," I muttered, fumbling in my bag for cash.

I thought about my grandma, who told me everyone deserves our compassion. Still, if she had actually made it to heaven I would've expected her to brag about her fate by sending me a rainbow or something.

Thinking about God on my morning commute proved unpleasant, so I tried to listen to the news instead, the familiar drone of Midwestern voices talking about climate change and foreign affairs. By the time I got off at my stop I'd learned something about Canada's oil supply, but I couldn't remember what. I flipped past a text from my mom asking to talk on the phone sometime soon. After the nightmare I wanted some peace—or at least free dissociation time.

I walked into my office. I worked at a kids' clothing store in Tribeca, so the office was a back room full of pests. At night I heard rats chewing through the copper wiring.

Little denim overalls and floral dresses hung in neat rows. Technicolor toys, gadgets, and gizmos glistened on white tables. My boss was stirring a spider into her coffee, watching its legs dissolve like pepper. She wore a shirt that said FEMALE SMALL BUSINESS OWNER in red Arial font. I think pink would've been offensive.

Pink was out. Girls like STEM now. Girls are small business owners. Girls run cults. Girls write true crime. Girls are vice presidents in pantsuits. Just not pink ones. I like wearing pink. And purple. There's a certain shade of purple I'm desperately looking for. I want it so bad it's almost a craving. There's joy in seeking out a certain pleasure and finding that it does indeed taste just like you imagined it would. Crafting an outfit you spend weeks putting together, tripping for the first time on good acid, sending a punishing text to someone who's hurt you, finding the book you've been looking for on a dusty shelf at East Village Books. New joy isn't static, it expands like lilac-colored slime. Almost lilac, but not quite. It's not exactly that pale Easter egg shade of purple girls wear to their yearly Episcopal outings. The problem is that it's not a color, it's a feeling.

"We need an extra pair of keys," my boss said without looking up from her laptop. It had a neon-green SHOP LOCAL sticker on the back.

One night a sleep paralysis demon had assumed the form of my boss. But she was just as scary in real life, considering she was an incompetent person who handled payroll. Sometimes she forgot to pay me. Other times she made me repeat my deadname over the phone, crowing like a vulture.

"Who are the keys for?"

"The repair man. Did you hear about the oil supply in Canada?"

"I was just listening to something about that on my subway ride," I said.

"Oh god, was the commute awful?" she asked.

"I'll be back soon," I said, dull-eyed and bleary from the ketamine.

I set out for the farther hardware store with the cute cashier.

The streets of Tribeca are trashier than you would expect. It's just the stores that are nice, and the neat little cafés with minimalist logos.

A man yelled something and laughed as he walked by me, but I didn't hear him. My headphones were maxed out. Some woman was screaming about shadowboxing her ex-lover, rolling around in the dirt and facing her inner demons. I loved women who could wrestle their darkness into words.

I couldn't find the right words. My dream had been to be

a journalist like all the other Hot Freelance Girls, but then I gave up. I did not want to think a single thought ever again. For a while I pursued a pure holy feeling—like doing K in the bathroom while wearing a leopard-print tube top. After a year of Bimboism, I got rid of my chokers and bought turtlenecks. I wore all black and monochrome baby doll outfits in an attempt to mimic the Trans-Girl Actress. God willing. I stopped reading anything contemporary. I wanted to become a premenopausal spinster. I spent hours reading classics in my shitty armchair and petting a foster cat. Anything long and tedious where women get punished. I didn't dare post about it. Pretentious, I heard the reply guys in my head. I read sweet poems to try to feel better. I tried so hard to forget the Bible verses my mom had taught me. The silly, comforting verses and hymnals I used to erase queer feelings. Now they mocked me. Exodus had that thing about men in dresses. I lost the soothing power of poetry. I wanted a little answer to life's wartime mystery. Instead my mind was cluttered by scraps of theology mixed with political social media maxims.

5 Ways to Abolish the Cop in Your Head!

I'd love to. But He's very big and almighty and sometimes He wears a shepherd's costume when He appears in my room. The worst sleep paralysis demon was the biblically accurate angel. Millions of eyes orbiting around a single sphere blazing with frightful glory.

As I trudged around Tribeca, past trophy wives walking their children like dogs and auteurs sipping lattes, I tried not to think about my own mom. I was ignoring her texts just like my landlord's. The only texts I wanted to read were from men who called me their beautiful little slut. My phone beeped when I got to the crosswalk, and I checked to see who it was. By the time I looked up I was almost a pancake. I flipped off the BMW, but it had already charged ahead, swerving to avoid two kids with Gucci backpacks.

"I'll sue you!" a little girl in pigtails screamed.

Tribeca is a strange Charlie Brown cartoon. The kids really can sue you—or at least their celebrity-lawyer parents can.

Despite the daily recklessness I encountered, I had yet to see a car crash in New York. I'd crashed a car once. When I was sixteen, I walked out of conversion therapy and wrapped my mom's car around a telephone pole. My therapist had said it was harder to go straight once you'd tasted the forbidden fruit. Imagine it, the fuck worth eternal damnation.

The hardware man yelled across the store about drywall while he copied the keys. He didn't smile at me. The store smelled like mildew and steel, thousands of tools in plastic boxes and lots and lots of Spackle. When he waved me back to the counter, I saw him check out my tits. My boss got mad when I didn't wear a bra, but she never said anything, she just glared at them. It was too dangerous for her to verbalize. I knew I was supposed to butch it up just the right amount for her—if I looked too made-up she'd call me a gender traitor, but I'd be in equally hot water if I looked too manly. Balance is the key to everything, especially when you're trying not to get fired. That morning, it wasn't a choice, I just didn't have the energy to look through my laundry.

My friends warned me to turn the other cheek to misogyny, especially from other women. But whenever I got clocked by a joke I felt like I was being watched. How chill was I? How big was my claim on womanhood? When people said they hated women "as a joke," I looked nervous and shifted the conversation. When people said women were weak, I metabolized it, eroticized it, and kept moving. I think that made people believe I was kind.

My phone pinged again reminding me I hadn't read that text. It wasn't my landlord or my mom. It was my ex-girlfriend Ash. She was still one of my best friends, even if she lived in Indiana.

girl i'm literally begging you to
join the cause

i just watched three girls go down
on each other

this could all be yours for the low,
low cost of a plane ticket

Ash had started one of those all-trans rural communes. In college we had an on-again, off-again thing and I hadn't dated another trans girl since. My friend Hazel always said I was a repressed lesbian. None of my friends could understand what I saw in men.

The men I saw were carpenters, gamers, married, straight, bi, kinky, kind, cruel. I tried to stop asking questions after a while. They were all going to go home to beautiful women. Women with jobs and smooth arms and smooth thoughts. One of my exes was a freegan who taught me how to dumpster dive. Or tried to anyway. Mostly I picked at stale bagels for a week before realizing he never texted me first. Each failed lover spurred me to reexamine my skin-care routine. I walked through wind tunnels formed by huge towers hunting for high-end moisturizers. Every time I tried out a new mud mask, the Tribeca moms complimented me on my glow.

Ash sent a picture of two trans girls in latex bondage gear feeling each other up against a giant oak tree.

this is the future trans anarchists
want

I didn't realize her commune had any political affiliation. I looked closer and realized there was a deer strung up behind them.

Miss u babe

Her life took place on a different shore than mine. Everything and everyone moved for her like Moses parting the Red Sea. When people stared at her on the street she turned to them and said, "Hello!" with sunny Midwestern aggression. Meanwhile I spent hours scrolling past the Hot Freelance Girls, wishing I had their bodies and copying their diets: black coffee, apple, banana, oatmeal. A stolen salad from Whole Foods. As I bit into my banana, I scrolled my phone to see if I'd updated my grocery list. I made and deleted lists. Lists of faults, accomplishments, things to do, books read, books to read, the worst fruits, cosmetics to try. I checked them to soothe myself. Once I listed everyone who had cum inside me. It was a short list: my rapist.

I thought it was funny. My ex Ryan hated it. He was the kind of Brooklyn white guy to react if you critiqued the micro-identity he'd carefully formed through years of scrolling. He downplayed his Supreme addiction in favor of Male Feminist discourse, David Lynch's coffee line, and Roberto Bolaño's "complicated engagement with femicide and surrealism." He asked me to go to Film Forum a few times a month and as much as I enjoyed a seven-hour movie, I usually tried to find an excuse not to.

"We should go camping sometime," he said once.

"What will you do when we run out of IPA?" I replied.

He didn't talk to me for an hour after that. Then I went down on him and ignored the tranny porn he put on in the background. He was kind of ugly in a way that made cis girls afraid of him, but I didn't have anything better going on. I was a good fixer though, so we carried on for a while. Eventually Ryan called me a misandrist after I told him the porn he watched was kinda fucked-up. If I was a misandrist, why did I want a husband so badly? We broke up when he moved to San Diego to work for a tech firm. After he left, I karaoked Joni Mitchell songs and my friend Xiomara held my hair back in the bathroom. Then I dated the freegan, then a boring NYU twink who took me to terrible plays about climate change. We ate ramen in silence, and he walked too far ahead of me. Afterward, I started hooking up with trans guys. Sometimes when they texted me to hook up, they asked how I was feeling first.

As I walked the rest of the way back to the store, I thought about the time Ash fingered me in a gas station bathroom off the I-5.

I realized too late how long I had been wandering around Tribeca staring at stray cats. When I walked back in the store my boss gave me a disgruntled sigh. I played with a tiny toy drum and gave her a half-hearted smile.

"Got the keys," I said.

"I'm going to the bank," she said. "And I'm getting a salad. I think I'm just gonna take a long lunch."

As soon as she was out the door, her strappy sandals clicking on the sidewalk, I opened the store computer, signed into my email, and tried to write. It was my favorite thing, journaling about the depression walks I took in search of hazelnut coffee. My friends did not tell me the things I wrote were good, but they did say congratulations with the strained voices of people bored at a party. I thought I understood the college graduates who cynically moved in and out of the city, kissed one another on rooftops, never invited me out, and fought for the same three entry-level media jobs. I looked down on them. It was easy to be principled when no one was offering me anything.

I was debating whether or not to take a babysitting gig when my boss came back in with a soy matcha latte. The foam was full of shredded psychoactive mushroom bits swimming around like ancient ocean bacteria. Almost no one had come in all day. I spent most of my time reading about the Famous Trans-Girl Actress's affair with a married cis man.

"Well. How'd we do?" she asked, tapping her nails on the plastic lid of her drink. I could tell by the way she grasped the cup that something was off.

"Fine. Not too many people came in."

"How many?"

"I didn't count," I lied. She wouldn't like the answer.

She sighed and sat down on a pink metal chair. "I think we're going to have to close."

"What?" I jerked.

"We haven't had that many sales. The pipes in the basement burst. I can't afford it."

There had been no warning, no indication. Every so often my paycheck was a few days late, but that was beyond normal. Just how things went in bureaucratic America.

"How much do you have in the bank?"

"I don't have enough for payroll." My boss looked over at me with a single tear in her eye. Her icy demeanor melted into a heroic display of grief. She started apologizing, hysterically fighting back sobs. "It's just such a bad time—and I know this is awful. I have to think of my kid, I have to make sure everything goes well for her."

"For *her*," I said.

I thought about flashing my tits but merely flipped her off instead. She wasn't worth it. I stormed out and called Hazel, furious at the indecency of my boss. I was the aggrieved party, I was the one who would struggle.

"I just got fired."

"What?"

"I got fired," I yelled into the receiver. The heat of my anger surprised me.

"Jesus," she said. "Well let's go out. Blow off steam."

"I don't want to go out, I don't know what I'm gonna do, babe. I don't have any money. Not really."

"Let's meet up tonight, I love you, I'll send you the party details."

She hung up before I could say more. I loved her but she wasn't always a feelings person. She liked to do.

None of my friends had stable careers, but Hazel sometimes showed her work at galleries and got invited to things. Hazel made horrific, many-eyed plastic dolls with crow feet and sold them to the girls. Sometimes she made fuzzy abstract paintings and we all trudged through the rain and sleet, under the J train and past the McDonald's, to go look at them. I would grab a giant Diet Coke and sip it in a lavender velour hoodie as I stared blankly at her work.

I already knew what Hazel would say about Ash texting me again. Though they'd never met, everyone knew about the riptide she created in me. I was always in Ash's current, wondering what type of trans-girl nation she would build. Like Charon, she would ferry me across the Styx and I would let her usher me into paradise. Even hundreds of miles away, she called to me like a siren. I thought she would feel like home forever. She was always the one who helped me carefully craft texts back to my mom whenever I didn't go back for Christmas.

I spent the afternoon looking at flyers in a park, calculating how long I could last without a steady paycheck. Not long. I couldn't ask my mother for money, I didn't have the allure or stamina it took to do cam work, and I wasn't sure I had anything valuable to sell. Not eating seemed like a bad option and would probably only make the money last slightly longer. Female-run business, they said, it will be less transphobic. You're less likely to get fucked over. I didn't want to look for a new job. Much less learn to please someone else's punishing sensibility. I texted a few of the Tribeca moms I babysat for, hoping someone needed something that day.

The "all good for today but . . ." texts trickled in as I sat on a park bench watching a gray bush of feathers stumble around pecking at crumbs. Beside me was a coughing older man eating a bacon, egg, and cheese. A group of kids walked by on their way to kindergarten. The teachers had them leashed together like reindeer. On Tommy, on Kaiden, on Arcadia. One mom ended up asking me if I could pick up her hair dye. On the way back to her house I looked at her Amex receipt. It was over a hundred dollars.

I wished I had another bodega coffee. I love awful sugar replacements, stevia and aspartame are addictive. An old woman in a pink Chanel suit was dropping sunflower-seed kernels for the pigeons across from me. We were in a competition. Her lipstick was a little off, so she looked like a clown too. She was a prune. A pink bouffant prune-shaped clown.

By four I was optimistic. I resolved to get fucked. It'd been a minute. Sex always seemed like the magic release valve. I decided to reach back out to Max. He didn't do a lot during the day. I wasn't even sure what he did at night. Something carpentry related. We got together after the boring freegan and I broke up, so I had low expectations.

u around?

hey babe what's up? just going down a Wikipedia hole on dogfighting

of course

i'm a little wet

i was thinking about the last time i saw u

you better be wet for me

why don't u come over in an hour?

An hour later we were on Max's roof. I saw the gray mirage swaying below us. In the distance I saw Manhattan, each tower an icon for some big banking company.

I'd dressed up. I was wearing black lace thigh highs and combat boots. A short black PVC skirt, no bra, and a thin red shirt. I'd toned down the makeup. I wasn't trying to go overboard, just suggest the part I was playing.

"You look nice," Max said.

"How nice?"

Max got close to me and knocked me down to the floor. I forgot how strong he was. He started biting my neck like a crocodile before working his way to my tits and then commanding me to take off my blouse. As I flipped it over my head, my tits slipped out and he smiled devilishly, squeezing them in his hands before looking for the flogger he'd discreetly brought up with him. He showed it to me, asking, pleading.

"Sure."

I liked seeing my tits turn into a red mess. If he had anything to tie me up with I would've requested that too but he wasn't a proper dom. Max had me get on my knees. It was time to shake my ass. I briefly wondered if the neighbors would hear before I gave in and yelped.

"Yes, baby."

It was his turn to be serviced. He facefucked me while I was on the ground. It didn't last that long—he didn't wait to cum before sliding my legs over his shoulders and burying me in his mouth. I was over it long before he was. Good pussy doesn't dissociate.

"Hey I think I'm okay . . ."

I guess he didn't hear me, he was moaning so loud. Sex, I know personally, is not about thinking. It's an ego death, sure, but in the most selfish way possible. When people describe the feeling as *pure*, they're trying to stretch their vocabulary to find another word for *dissolve*. It doesn't happen every time. But sometimes I can turn into the same white noise I listen to when I fall asleep.

"You serve our community," Max said when I'd told him I mostly fucked trans guys.

Ryan never said things like that. He was a menace. On our first date, I brought Max the weird energy drink he liked and played with his gecko. Trans guys always had weird pets. It was hot to me. Whenever I tried to date another girl she just asked for yerba maté and tried to show me noise music in her impossibly messy room.

I was drifting in and out of my body. He didn't know what he was doing. I'd miscalculated. His roof was crammed full of potted plants. Wildflowers, browning ferns, and an empty birdcage. He didn't seem like a florist but maybe his roommate or one of the other tenants had the green thumb. I couldn't focus on what he was doing. I felt ticklish. His mouth scratched like gravel. I wanted to dig. I got him to switch to hand stuff using a gentle tug.

"Are you gonna be a good girl for me?"

He wanted me to finish. Misogyny is expecting too much of a woman. Feeling no better, I was forced to explain dissociation pussy to Max.

"I've been really out of it lately," I said. "It's like I can feel something bad is going to happen."

I picked at a forget-me-not, mashing the blue petals into a gritty paste.

"Are you okay?"

"Yeah. Why wouldn't I be?"

"Should I, like . . . walk you to the subway?"

It was probably better that I didn't sleep over—no room at the inn and his room was a mess of tattoo-gun needles and ramen packets—but the offer still would've been nice.

"No, it's fine. I can get there on my own."

I walked to the subway. I heard motorcycles in the distance. Sex had to taste like metal to be good. Or that's what I told myself to get over my inability to get wet. When Ryan and I were together he always wanted me to take Viagra. It worked a little, but it made me feel like shit. Stuff like that made my vision crimson.

While I was alone on the platform, Max sent me an apologetic breakup text. Even though we'd only hung out twice he'd framed it explicitly as a hard ending.

"Fuck that," I yelled.

I didn't even care about him. I wanted to get dicked down and score a free meal and instead ended up bagging a feelings text. I had no feelings. I boiled them down in an inner well of resilience. Trans girls are immune to criticism. Not because we're superhuman but because we have already been criticized into the margins. I have no heart, just a bunch of cybernetic mixtapes and failed Grindr hookups stitched together in the shape of one.

Last Valentine's Day, a few weeks after me and Ryan broke up, I saw a guy who dressed me in a rubber suit and edged me.

Edging isn't very fun when you already barely cum. When I tried to leave, he started telling me about his band. Somehow every cis dude has a math-rock band and thinks their record will "get you into it." It's impossible to say you just came over to cum. If I could order a McOrgasm I would. Instead I am attempting to garner connections to DJs and vagabonds. Don't get me wrong, I love the right kind of vagabond. Maybe Ash's promised land would hit the right spot. Maybe giving in was the right move. There was something about her.

The subway still hadn't come, but the tracks were moving like a smooth, silver river. I tried to look closer but couldn't make out what kind of trick the light was playing. I heard the train coming as I saw through the light beams. Snakes. A river of silver snakes moving toward the other mouth of the tunnel. I heard them screaming as the train screeched to a halt and slid open for me.

Ash sent a voice note. She was going to wear me down until I responded.

"We're *not* a cult. It's nothing like what you went through. We're not dogmatic. We're all about creating a separate freedom. We just got a cow actually. One of the girls here got a license to carry and started teaching us how to shoot."

I wondered how one milked a cow. Then I thought about how my mom always told me that I should learn how to shoot. She started bugging me about it after the Pulse massacre. I dreamed of trans women showering together and licking AK-47s. Too many people were crowding my daydream. Pushing clowns, angels, and moms out of the way, I typed a message back to Ash.

I miss you too babe

TRIP SERMON

By the time I met up with Hazel later that night, our friends Xiomara and Nora had gone home, deciding it was long past their bedtime and nothing good could come from staying out. Hazel agreed but pressed on. She was trying to top the last time she did Molly and saw a ghost who asked her what year it was. I kept checking my phone, which annoyed Hazel to no end. Romantic progression felt like the only way to move my life forward.

"I asked her what time she was from. She said 2066. I told her she went back in time . . ."

The rave was dying down. I wasn't high enough for Hazel's trip sermon. She was one of those trans girls who believed in transcestors. We went outside to smoke with the other trans girls at the party. I was ignoring a text from Ash about how the trans girls I hung out with didn't know how to practice solidarity. That *I* didn't know how to practice solidarity.

"Do you have a light?"

The girl to my right, Arrow, was a figurehead in the New York trans-girl community. She was a model/poet who frequently "hosted" parties like this one. She was tall and lithe with perfectly lined pouty lips, and wearing a skimpy white dress. Her tits were huge, her hair dyed an infernal red.

I handed her my lighter. She accepted it and lit her cigarette. Another trans girl beside her quickly snatched it to light her own. I'd followed these girls for years, but they still didn't know who I was. I didn't wear my jealousy well. It felt easier to mark trans women as either safe or dangerous. Arrow was definitely the latter. If I hadn't met Ash pretransition, she probably would've been dangerous too. Girls like Hazel and Xiomara didn't scare me because they wore their desires on their sleeves. Arrow acted like she was above it all. And in a way she was. I didn't feel the need to act in solidarity with her.

"What?" the girl next to Arrow asked after she caught me staring.

"Nothing," I said.

A few boys came out and walked over to Arrow and her friend. I turned back to Hazel, deciding my lighter wasn't worth it.

"Let's go home," I begged.

"I think in another life, I would've been a really famous artist."

"Totally," I said.

I tried to find a way to switch topics. I didn't want to confirm or deny her sinking suspicions that her work was derivative. I decided to stop trying to convince her to go home and dragged her back onto the dance floor. Arrow gave us a poisonous look as we walked back inside.

It was almost two in the morning. The lights flashed a disorienting violet color. Somewhere the sound of a sink echoed loudly, part of the ambient musician's new song. God forbid a song with a melody came on. My loyalty to trans-girl musicians was wavering. Sometimes I really did want to hear a rambling man plucking his guitar. The sink sound turned into boiling water. Hazel was yelling in my ear, her mouth hot with fury.

"I just love *us*. I love *women*."

She wanted to make out. I didn't.

"I have to go to the bathroom," I said.

Even if the Molly wasn't a dud, it wasn't having any effect on me. It was the third time I'd tried in three months. I walked to the bathroom and sat on the toilet pondering how much longer I could last before I called a cab and dragged Hazel with me. Once she found a new mark, she would vanish on me, only reappearing the next time she was single. She was a girlfriend girl.

The girl in the next stall over asked if I had a tampon.

"I'm sorry, no."

"Are you sure?"

"Yes."

By the time the girl left, I had scrolled through an entire article about the exact year New York would be plunged underwater due to climate change. It seemed like we were all getting a raw deal. In just a matter of decades we would be alone in the universe, moving toward global glacial disaster. Overnight oats were nothing against encroaching deforestation and islands of dead seals. Meal prep and nihilism were closing in on each other. Okay, I told myself. Abort.

When I walked out I realized there was something weird streaking the mirror. I hated looking at my reflection anyway. The sink was bubbling with yellow pus, craggy with white tufts of something I couldn't place. Pills maybe. There was no more soap.

I had goose bumps. It was colder in the bathroom than I'd expected. Usually they were packed with thrill seekers intent on finding body heat, but now the lavatory was eerily empty. I heard a dripping sound.

If I were smart, I would've turned around and left. But I was not smart. Instead I lit a joint and tried to drown out my uneasiness. I'd been practicing my whole life—every time I fucked, whenever I went to work or to the endless medical appointments where my deadname swung from the rafters.

Being trans is a logistical nightmare. I used to wonder why other trans people seemed so scattered. My Taurus moon wasn't in love with their flighty, messy, late vibes. But then I too started showing up late to functions. There's too much to keep track of. I can never remember to bring all my meds, all my documents, all my accessories, all my makeup. I leave behind a little scavenger hunt for my estrogen-confused brain.

Sometimes I complained about the temperature to cis women, and they joked along.

"No," I told them, "I'm on hormones."

It wasn't like they didn't know, they just refused to say it out loud. I wanted them to suffer a little too, even if just for a moment, at a tacky bar with yellow neon and a scratched-up pool table.

My feet slipped. The floor was covered in goop. I felt my back slam hard into the slime.

"Evil, evil girl."

I didn't see anyone in the bathroom. Only empty stalls filling with goo. I tried to get up but kept slipping.

"Bad girls get punished."

The voice seemed to come from nowhere, a disembodied shadow crossing over the dark windows and mirrors. I told myself it couldn't be that bad if the windows hadn't shattered. The voice was almost cartoonishly ghoul-like, a parody of horror-movie tropes. Even if I'd heard it before, it was jarring all the same.

"Bad, bad girls!"

"You need a new line," I attempted in a shaky voice.

The ooze around me seemed a little less sticky for a moment. Music penetrated the bathroom walls again. Whatever presence had touched our realm seemed to have gone. I caught my breath.

"Evil, evil girl."

My throat felt sore, scratchy, and tender. My mouth held the faint taste of metal. My sight was patchy. Something shuffled in the only bathroom stall that was closed.

"Who's there?"

The noise stopped.

I reached into my handbag and found the little capsule of oil I kept on hand in case of emergencies. The ground wouldn't work, it was covered in muck. I would have to get to the mirror a few feet away.

Demonology had become a bit of a pet hobby over the years. I was no expert, but I knew the major classification distinctions and some basic banishing techniques. Unfortunately most of them were based in the Christian tradition, so I was forced to revive some of my childhood mysticism. I never saw angels, only demons. Sometimes, when I was really scared, I mouthed the prayers my grandma had taught me.

But this was beyond anything I'd ever seen. I wasn't at home, I wasn't drifting in and out of sleep, and I couldn't pretend it was merely a nightmare. This was something new.

"How's it going in there?" I asked.

"You don't know anything," the voice repeated.

My ears were ringing, vertigo overtook me as I struggled to keep upright. After a minute my hands found the goopy floor and I was able to steady myself. I felt dirty. Like a slut, a whore, a little tranny girl. The image I saw of myself as a brick.

"Shut up," I muttered to the void. The demon's attention was pricked. "Are you trying to hurt me?"

"I am no one. I am a fragment of what's to come."

I stumbled to the mirror, flailing with my little vial of oil.

"What's going to come? More like you?"

"The end, the end," the voice echoed.

"Isn't it always? If it isn't climate change, it'll be the apocalypse," I said as I dabbed the oil onto my finger and steadied myself against the sink.

My mind was screaming in pain, as if the demon and I were directly linked. I couldn't admit to myself how terrified I was, that he was stronger than what I usually saw—little gremlins of the night or shadowy spirits easily cast out by a simple heavenly utterance.

"The end of what?" I asked as my finger hovered over the mirror.

"*You.* The whores of Babylon," a whisper behind me answered.

I could feel his cool breath on my skin, could see a single red eye and the contours of a pristine suit in the mirror as I quickly drew a cross on the glass, screaming as I did.

Solitude.

I was alone on all fours in a very normal-looking bathroom, dangerously close to a patch of puke, but otherwise unharmed. Still the reverberation of evil lingered. Someone walked in and asked if I was okay. They must have heard my scream. Saying nothing, I ran past her without looking back.

On the dance floor, I stared at Hazel. Alone, swaying like a branch. Her hair clung in clumps against her rosy, sweaty forehead. She had stripped down to a sports bra and jeans. It struck me that she was one of the few people I knew without any tattoos. In another story, in another little girl's fairy tale, we would've gotten together that night and slept soundly in each other's arms. We would've made pancakes and gotten stable jobs. That was some other trans girl's escape chute. It wasn't mine. I chose to be willfully ignorant of her horny maneuvers.

Evil. Evil girl.

Everyone thinks they have a story to tell.

Why me?

God hates me.

Everyone has a theory about their story too. I try to avoid my own. Instead I have a theory about King David. I think he was in love with his best friend Jonathan. Fags. They were best friends according to the Bible, two men who spurred each other to love God. But in my version, their wives were jealous and tried to keep them in line. Besides, neither of the men were very good at guilt. They should've worked on that. It would've made for a better ending. The two gays learn self-forgiveness and leave their country behind for the wicked hills of Canaan. Instead, David hides out in caves. Nobody talks much about what happened to poor old Jonathan.

"I'm gonna go," I said when I got close enough to Hazel that she could hear me.

She looked at me like I'd betrayed her fundamental right to party.

"You're . . . gonna . . . go?"

"I've seen all there is to see here."

"Okay."

She looked at me expectantly. I was supposed to invite her to get food or take her home. She was my friend.

"You want me to call us a car?" I asked.

The music picked up again. I could barely hear her response.

"I'm gonna stay!"

"Will you be okay?"

Hazel nodded and pointed to another girl near her. Thumbs-up, all clear. A point was being made. I was a prick.

I laid my head down just as the clock struck three. The hour of the wolf. It was, according to the only exorcist I knew, the time when demons roamed free looking for easy prey. I was about as easy as it got.

"Demons go away in the name of the Lord Jesus Christ," I mumbled quietly. It was something my grandmother had taught me when things were really bad.

My mom was the one who originally encouraged me to join an experimental therapeutic group that specialized in helping people like me. It was later described in the local paper as a cult—by Evangelicals, so you knew it was a *cult* cult. That was how I started seeing my conversion therapist. God didn't care. He watched me face it without a drink in my hand. Not that I was drinking at that age—I was much too goody-goody. My conversion therapist welcomed me without so much as a cup of coffee. We sat crisscross applesauce on the ground and talked about God, my dad, whether or not I enjoyed baseball for the right reasons. Once, I made the mistake of bringing a Nietzsche book with me. Bill, who had me call him by his first name, told me Nietzsche didn't believe in art.

"Don't you believe in art?" he asked.

"Of course," I said.

"Then why are you reading Nietzsche?"

Whenever I read my journal from that time I see the fraying crazy girl I could've been. Anyone who wants to be a poet should be forced to hide every poem they write for ten years and then decide if it is still worth publishing. I've told all my friends they can just burn my journals when I'm gone.

Conversion therapy was presented as a healing program. I would become whole again, washed clean in God's eyes. I would feel worthy. I would remember life was worth living. Loneliness would become obsolete, a magic bullet cure for a girl on the edge.

The business of change is a tricky thing. So many want it so badly. For a while I too believed I could change. I believed sexuality wasn't fixed. I could become an ex-gay. Freedom meant freedom from sin, not freedom to sin. Then later, in order to cope, I decided it was fixed and that meant I was not a sinful gay but a natural gay. Now, yet again, I'm less convinced sexuality is fixed. Why does it need to be? I can have my pussy and eat it too.

I couldn't prove to anyone that my life would always be happy. I couldn't prove anything except that life could either be possibly worth living or not worth living at all. Some things just happen and we're drawn toward them with the power of inevitability. Some girls I know talk about the process of starting hormones as if in a trance, continually saying they aren't sure even as they google doctors, watch YouTube videos, make appointments, take their first injections. It's not simply that the body knows before we do—the body can't act alone, though perhaps it can override our hesitation. We followed the hypnosis of need.

Being a closeted teen girl was hoping one day you too would have a pregnancy scare while driving your cis girlfriends to get Plan B. We hid our nocturnal activities from our parents, knowing the possible punishments that awaited us. We talked about escape and got high and sat down on the tennis courts at three in the morning. All the books we read about teenagers made us think that our experiences with love would matter later on—that hurt could be overcome with language. We lived in the shadow of feminism's belief in talk therapy. So we talked. We figured we could work through anything with one another. We went on long walks around the neighborhood because we couldn't stand still. We told one another we would move and make something of ourselves. I tried to convince everyone over fruity wine that we had lives worth living, that movies about kids with fucked-up brains were too romantic, even if they got one thing right. It did feel like life and death. When you get older, you forget that part. In high school, it felt urgent like a knife. It felt like everyone was only two steps away from the psych ward. Some of us did our stints. I could still remember setting off fireworks in baseball fields, staring at the waning moon, and walking home in a stupor. I don't think any of us had therapists, not real ones anyway, not until much later. How old do you have to be to confront your childhood?

The TV in my room turned to static. Outside police sirens cooed. I didn't want to have any dreams that night. I started writing a text to Ash about what I'd just seen but stopped. There was nothing I could say that would make her understand. So I looked through the photos she'd posted until I found one of us back from when I'd taken care of her during bottom surgery. We were beneath a bright-blue tarp and she was holding up a used dilator that I had drawn a smiley face on.

"Blood sisters," the caption read.

MY FAVORITE EXORCISM

Hazel ended up getting us into a Women in the Arts brunch for free. Someone had seen one of her dolls at a gallery in Red Hook and dubbed her a modern-day Greer Lankton. I didn't really want to go out again, but after my brush with the demonic, I also didn't want to be alone. I chose the lesser of two evils.

No matter where I looked I saw shadows crisscrossing in front of me, morphing into humanoid shapes. I felt like something was following me, like the presence I saw in the bathroom was going to return at any moment and terrorize me with its glaring red eye. I didn't know what to tell the girls. They wouldn't believe me. All my life I'd been sensitive to the spiritual but never knew how to explain it to my friends. Everyone else seemed to live free from guilt and ghouls. A double life, framed by discussions of hauntings and warehouse parties.

"I'm nothing like Greer," Hazel said, though we all knew she was secretly pleased. We walked down into the subway as she briefed us on her night at the club. I stayed quiet. No one asked me how my night went. Maybe they realized I was feeling sensitive and left it at that. She smiled the whole ride into Manhattan. Hazel's emotional-support ex, Nora, was chugging a Pedialyte as we emerged into the glaring white summer morning. I tried to engage her in conversation, but she was monosyllabic. Meanwhile, Xiomara was texting a girl she'd started flirting with on the internet. I'd have to wait for her to come back down to earth. I texted Ash.

everyone's so wrapped up
in themselves

they're getting in their own way

when you're around so many cis
people it can be easy to lose your
way

accolades from cis people are a
distraction

we have to build it ourselves

yeah yeah . . .

at least xiomara is trying to find
another woman to make a life with

this one's cis apparently lol

[eye-roll emoji]

I looked over at my friends. Hazel was telling a disinterested Nora about a curator she was hoping to see at the brunch. I finished my bodega coffee and threw the cup in the trash as we walked the rest of the block.

The old four-story brick building looked out of place amid the steel towers and midrange salad bars. Ivy grew over its walls, hiding the original placard that no doubt claimed a revolutionary lineage.

"It used to be an old church," Hazel told us as we walked past an usher into the strange-smelling foyer.

We passed a giant mural of the Virgin Mary as we climbed the steps to the main hall. I could smell the thick sweat of maple syrup and bacon. A massive banquet dominated the corridor. Cis women with smug grins and tacky pearls gabbed while downing white wine. Schubert played quietly in the background.

"My New York success story . . ."

A few white women buzzed around the bar and smoothed their dresses as we waited for the keynote speaker. Myself a failed white woman, I wondered if I was ever going to have a New York success story. Perhaps I shouldn't want one. I'd tried so hard to be a writer only to discover no one made money as a writer anymore, they only cycled through credit, debt, and smaller and smaller apartments. Successful writers were always optimistic, they told you to go for it. Failed ones told you tenderly that it was okay to fail. I watched the Hot Freelance Girls in the back of the restaurant sniffing free martinis and sneaking granola bars into their bags. After all the clickbait blogs had fallen, they circled every event hoping to land a book deal. Memoir was code for "give me a TV deal please." Everyone in New York had a pilot, just like in L.A. I wanted the life they had. My gaze dripped with murderous envy.

Hazel came walking up behind me humming Radiohead, something about bodies. I jumped as her hands grazed my shoulders.

"Lighten up, girl," Hazel said.

"Fuck off," I said, trying to smile and make it seem like a lighthearted joke. No dice. She could tell I was on edge.

Deep breath. List favorite writers. List food eaten today. List past mistakes. Let go. List them all again an hour later. I thought of all the articles the Hot Freelance Girls had written.

How I Learned to Love Gay-for-Pay Porn as a Lesbian

The Polyamorous Professor Who Married Her Student

How Ketamine Is Ruining the Trans Community's Ability to Organize

A Look into the Lives of Trans Teens in Florida

Library Bans Are No Joke. We Need Sober Queer Spaces.

BookTok Is Killing Goodreads. Here's Why That's a Good Thing.

We're Thinking About Mental Health All Wrong

Can Contemporary Fiction Be Good? A Case Study

I Know My Sister's Ugly

Ernest Hemingway Was a Trans Woman. Prove Me Wrong.

And, of course, the profile on Hazel: *This Trans Artist Is Following in the Footsteps of Doll Maker Greer Lankton*

For some reason the headlines were always a million words long. While I was watching the Hot Freelance Girls out of the corner of my eye, one of them tried talking to Nora. She had more cachet than I did and she didn't even care. She was a small-time celebrity because she DJed a party the Trans-Girl Actress frequented.

Things weren't clicking into focus for me. Everywhere I looked there were more women, all just silhouettes waltzing around in tropical-colored dresses. The room was painted a taupey-cream color. The peach tablecloths were crowned with zinnia-and-sunflower centerpieces. I counted the trans girls in the room. Besides me and my friends I saw maybe one or two. Unless they weren't as clocky as us, which was certainly possible. I kept saving up for a pussy but couldn't seem to make it past a few thousand without something befalling me or someone I loved. There was always another GoFundMe.

New content. I was trying to feel the thrill of new content, I remembered. New feelings, new vibes. I didn't want to ruminate on my life like a hummingbird hypnotized by the only feeder in the cul-de-sac. I wanted to go somewhere outside the zoning grid of my brain. That was why I'd come to New York—to start over. To get away from the religious zealotry of my old life. Not to fall right back into the abyss.

I took a sip of wine and looked at my friends. We were not the most glamorous Women in the Arts. Xiomara was talking to someone who had recently been published on the annoying website funded by an arms dealer and joined the ranks of canceled artists and postfeminist theorists. Not that there was anywhere moral to write for anymore. That was another reason Ash told me to leave. "Culture can't come from within the center. It comes from the margins."

We were tourists after all, Xiomara reminded us. She was the only one who spoke Spanish, chatting with the women getting their carts ready or the Dominican men at the bodega. Xiomara's aunt lived in the city, and even though they were on difficult terms, she often went over for Sunday dinners. Sometimes she liked to drink a beer or two with us when she got back and tell us about her family. The rest of us were too afraid to talk about our families. My life beyond the city was background noise. Xiomara was the only one to ever ask me about it. She asked me to explain things I had barely begun to think about for myself. Many of my friends in the city came from places they tried to forget—sometimes embarrassingly so. Some tried to forget abuse and some tried to forget wealth. Some both.

Nora grabbed a beer and walked past Hazel, who had found the curator she wanted to talk to. They were touching each other's shoulders in a knowing way. God love her, she didn't have a lot of rules or self-respect. Hazel let Nora follow her around and sulk. I think she enjoyed having hangers-on. Nora was particularly alluring because she used to live in Berlin. The fact she didn't talk about her past made her an asset, someone along for the ride. As far as I knew she hadn't fucked anyone since the breakup, even though Hazel clearly had. That was almost two years ago. The curator touched Hazel's thigh and I averted my gaze. Two of the Hot Freelance Girls waltzed past in perfect color-block dresses and square-toe heels. I went to grab a drink and listen in.

"I got ghosted by the *Times*, but *Vogue* got back to me and they're willing to do the cover story," the one with the Gucci ladybug purse said.

"My book-advance money is almost gone. My agent's trying to get me to pitch some shitty website to make a quick buck."

"At least you have an agent," the first one said.

They vanished into a cloud of Santal 33 and secondhand Prada. An older trans woman came up next to me at the open bar and ordered a mimosa. I remembered the recent profile in *New York Mag* about her. She had transitioned late in life, after traveling the world as a music reporter, trashing hotel rooms with the boys before landing a cushy job and book deal detailing her tour of Japan. Now she was making a comeback as an activist and travel writer.

"Hey, babe," she said. "Looks like you and your crew are the only other girls here."

"No," I said, pointing to the trans-girl journalist who had just reviewed a rap-country album for a big website. "She's a music writer. Does profiles. There's one or two others around here somewhere."

I didn't feel as starstruck as I expected. The woman seemed just as desperate as I did. She was carrying a big cell phone, a vape, and a pack of Marlboro Lights like Jenga blocks.

"Oh. Well. She your friend?"

"I've never talked to her."

"Are you a writer too," the woman said as she took a sip of her mimosa.

"Not really." I squirmed.

"Well, don't sweat it too much. It all comes out in the wash. I'm here too, aren't I? Life doesn't have to be beautiful. It can also be shitty and lonely when you risk it all and find out no one wants to fuck you except weird cis dudes in Jersey."

She took a long sip of her drink and smiled. I couldn't make sense of her tone, if she was sauced.

"Oh," I said.

"I'm kidding," she said. "I'm gay. I get all the pussy I want."

"I'm bi."

"I don't believe it. You have straight-girl vibes," she said eying me, her fingers pinching the thin stem of her glass. "When I transitioned, I stopped writing completely. For a year," she said. "Now I'm doing well. People invite me to bullshit like this."

We both knew I already knew that, but I didn't want to say so and prolong the conversation.

"Well."

I turned back to look at her. I knew I should summon some hero worship for her but she wasn't one of my idols. I thought she was perfectly fine. She was one of the few trans writers who hadn't tried to cash in on a memoir so I respected her more than others, but I also hadn't read her travelogue about Venice. We both surveyed the scene.

"They think because they're hot and write for *Vogue* they have more options," she said. "But I was never fuckable so I'll never be unfuckable. I'm just a forbidden dish somewhere on the buffet. Poisonous, like a puffer fish."

"I'm still trying to claw my way in," I replied.

A model/writer who'd recently interviewed a sculptor in Prague walked by me without saying hello. We'd met at least three times but she never remembered my name. I was just a puke-colored ghost to her. If only there were spells for that kind of a thing. Prosperity prayers or something. But God never seemed that interested in wealth. Not in my case anyway.

"The more you try to have a profound life, the sicker you'll feel," the woman said.

I took a long, meditative sip of my drink. She gave me a look before walking away that told me I couldn't trust anything she said. I tried to locate my girls in the crowd before it was too late. We'd been spending less time together and I wanted to go to a less chilly setting so we could dish. I realized if I didn't start the expedition, we wouldn't leave before we were too drunk to go anywhere else.

Excusing herself, the older woman went over to another group of writers all gossiping about something else I knew nothing about. Fine. I decided to try to sneak out for a cigarette.

My nerves were shot. I thought being in a room full of people would be a good idea but in reality there were no more good ideas. There were too many words, people, places, things. Maybe Ash had it right. I hated the way she tried to make her project a politic—a sort of go-back-to-the-land, trans-women-are-women type thing—but I knew as well as anyone there was a need for trans women to have their own spaces. I thought she'd gotten a little corny since our time together in college. Maybe New York just made me bitter, too afraid to let myself be happy.

The stairwell I found across from the reception wasn't the same one we'd climbed up on the way in but I figured the building couldn't be that large. It was humid with the dregs of summer air. I fanned myself a little before the lights snapped off.

"Hello?" I asked.

No answer. The red exit sign hung a few floors down. I could risk it and fumble my way down or just try to wait out the flickering darkness. Usually it only took me a day or two after a sleep paralysis dream to reset my nervous system. But now any encounter with the dark left me feeling shattered.

"Jesus fucking Christ," I hissed, desperately hoping the light would come back on soon and I would see Hazel at the top of the stairs with Nora and Xiomara. But I was alone again. They all had better things to do.

Instead I saw these strange vermillion orbs raining down from above like little embers. The spheres almost looked like fairy lights, but their coloring was off. Less inviting. I blinked to clear my vision and when I reopened my eyes, they were gone, leaving me once again in the unlit stairwell. I'd probably imagined them. Just a trick of the light. I was just more susceptible to believing in the otherworldly because of all my trauma. If I could afford EMDR, it would all go away. I took a deep breath and tried to recenter.

Then the orbs flashed again. This time, I saw them for what they were. Dozens of eyes with inky slits for irises. Out of the gloom I started to hear laughter too. A chorus of deep, distorted voices making fun of me. It all felt so real, like in a second the eyes would fly through my body, leaving behind craters in my flesh, and the voices would grow a body that could swing an axe. I screamed at the thought of my bloody death and nearly fell down the flight of stairs. Below me on the ground, a large emerald snake hissed, its body coiled tightly like a whirlpool of scales with gnashing fangs. I hated snakes. Growing up I even ran away from little garters in the field.

"This isn't real," I chanted, even as I felt the wet and mucusy sensation of something slithering over my hand. "Demons, go away in the name of the Lord—"

The door opened. A woman in a cream-colored slip dress and coral lipstick stared up at me. Before she had time to say anything, I bolted down the remaining stairs and ran out into the light. I caught my breath on the sidewalk in the bright afternoon sun, a few stray tears rolling down my cheeks, before sitting down on a bench in front of a Chase Bank and a bodega with an extravagant flower stand out front. I scrolled through the pictures Ash had posted since starting the commune. I needed to look at faraway places to dissociate.

"Herculine forever," Ash wrote under a pic of her surrounded by a dozen or so girls. I knew a few of them though I couldn't place how—Midwestern trans girls all seemed alike. Ash said most of them came to her like wounded butterflies, gorgeous creatures who needed a mother they kind of wanted to fuck. It did look a bit like utopia all of a sudden. I dialed her number and watched as a man watered the flowers. I stared at the hose showering the geraniums and orchids. The snapdragons were melting like a Crayola sunset.

"I bet you'll come here and fuck the love of your life," Ash said.

"I bet."

Birdsong and the skeletal shake of wind flooded the line. I heard Ash take a sip of something. I thought about the first time we had sex in college, in the late summer while lying on a tennis court, desperate for something else in the noisy twilight. We found a little corner where the spotlights couldn't reach. She tasted like cheap cinnamon gum and wet steel.

"You can stay as long as you like. We'll make it work."

"I don't have any money."

"No problem."

There wasn't any irony in what she said. I knew she would beg me if she thought it would work, but we both knew it wouldn't.

"Give me a day to think about it."

"You know the carrot will only look tastier."

"Your little trap."

"You'll love it. You miss me," Ash said.

"I do. I really do." The sun was finally starting to set. I looked at all my missed texts from Hazel and Xiomara. "What's it like out there?"

"The crickets are incredible. Like a choir. I can see the stars too. Like old times." Ash laughed.

"I remember."

"Don't you miss it? I missed nature a lot in Oakland. When I was recovering from surgery I just wanted to lie down in the grass and look up."

"You told me," I said. "You missed it a lot. I knew you wouldn't make it in a city."

We didn't say anything for a while. I could hear a whole menagerie of insects harmonizing.

"It's going to be a full moon tonight," she said after a while.

"Is it?"

"Babe. Come on. What's going on?"

"Nothing," I said. "I have nothing going on. I lost my job."

"Fuck . . . I'm sorry—"

"Oh shut up. We both know you're glad."

"No. I'm not," Ash said, even though I could practically hear her smiling.

"I don't have a job. I never even got to write."

"Bitch, you wrote that piece on Hazel's dolls."

"For free. I wrote it for free for an online-only bullshit paper."

"Okay," Ash said, quietly. "Go on crying then."

"I don't have a boyfriend," I said and heard her flinch. Ash would've preferred I said partner. "Ryan was a dud. A royal fuckup on my part to think he could've been anything. I don't have any prospects or even someone to give me the occasional orgasm. I can't save up for a pussy here. It's too expensive. I'm out of money as it is. I can't pay rent next month if I don't get a new bullshit job. And I just realized today I'm all out of ketamine."

The line went quiet for a while. When she came back, her voice sounded determined.

"How much money are you out?"

She made it sound like a choice. A cash infusion or a commune escapade.

"Ash, you're not fucking giving me money."

Fire truck sirens punctuated my declaration. I could've tried to mount a classic New York phoenix-from-the-ashes routine. Joust the Hot Freelance Girls. Get Medicaid. Get FFS. Ask Hazel or Xiomara to crash on their couch. But the truth was, I didn't want to. The demons and nightmares—it was too much. I needed an out. Maybe changing my geography would free me from the fear. Didn't they film *The Exorcist* in Brooklyn? I needed somewhere new, untainted by evil spirits, sleep paralysis, and slime demons. Rural Indiana seemed as good a place as any. Maybe it wouldn't change anything. Sure, I'd run anyway before—but not with Ash.

Part of me still thought she could save me. That love was a cure-all. I remembered the time we used to live together, how tranquil it was, how it felt so right. When we were together I never felt wrong in my body or soul. I felt like all those corny indie-rock love songs.

I sighed. "I'll come to Herculine. But only for a month. Or something. Then I have to come back. And I'll have to get a job."

"We can arrange that," Ash said immediately. There was no room to take a breath.

"How?"

"There'll be something for you when you get here. Do you trust me?"

Yes. I did.

"I'll be there by the end of the month."

"Perfect," she said. "I'll send you a pin. We're not on any map."

I laughed.

"What?" she asked.

"You're asking a lot of me," I said.

"Just like always," Ash said. "And you always come through, babe. We're fated."

"For what?"

"Hopefully we'll find out this time," she said.

The girls were back inside, huddled around Xiomara. Apparently she had gone on a date with a trans girl from Connecticut and they'd fucked in a park.

"She was sweet. I don't know if I'll see her again, but I had a nice time. Bit of a sob story."

"What was it this time?"

"Poor thing got kicked out and hasn't found a job yet. She's crashing with a friend, another girl, luckily."

"Fuck," I said.

"I mean look I get it, we all have our sad trans-girl sob story, but I don't want to hear about it on a first date," Hazel said.

"She was just very new to it all. I don't think that makes her a bad person, I just think it means she's looking for a mom, not a date," Xiomara said.

Ash's voice was infecting me. I could imagine her saying that Xiomara should've helped that girl find community instead of abandoning her to the harpies.

"Will you be her MILF?" Hazel poked.

"Absolutely not. I've done that too many times. It's not a good look for either of us."

"One day you'll have to settle down," Hazel said.

"The same goes for you," Xiomara said, sipping her drink. "How was the rave?"

"It was kinda shitty but I went home with this gorgeous fucking girl and we didn't sleep at all."

Nora looked up from her plate of waffles drenched in whipped cream and syrup. She seemed even quieter than usual.

"Are you gonna see her again?" I asked.

Hazel smiled before dropping her fork suddenly.

"Wait, I got the craziest email this morning. I can't believe I haven't told you all yet," she exclaimed. We waited with fearful eyes. "I have an audition."

"Whoa. Congrats. That's exciting, I know it's been a minute," I said, immediately worrying that it sounded like a slight. I thought of all the inspirational photos Hazel posted, complete with long captions reciting trans-girl affirmations.

"It's a sort of documentary-sitcom thing about dating while trans."

"Oh," Xiomara said.

"I feel like everyone in Hollywood's trying to launch the trans *Sex and the City*, but this may be it," Hazel said.

"You'll be everyone's wet dream."

"Yeah but I'm auditioning for this straight girl."

"When do you leave?" Nora asked.

"In a week."

"Congratulations," I said.

"Thank you," Hazel said as she finished her mimosa. I flinched, thinking about how soon my friend group would dissolve. *Sellouts,* I could practically hear Ash cooing in my ear.

"Wait, I have another party we should go to. It's some sort of opening," she said.

I looked back at my phone to see if Ash had texted me, giddy about my private decision. It felt like tanking my life, like taking control.

We left the Women in the Arts behind. On the way out, I stared at a mural of an angel bowing down to Mary. Sacrificial lamb in a blue cloak, giving up her ability to be seen in public as a decent woman by harboring an anarchist zealot. When I caught up to them, Hazel, Xiomara, and Nora were trying to find the last of the weed in their bags.

"I think I'm going to go to Ash's commune," I said when everyone was least on guard. I didn't want to have to explain myself to them.

"Did you get to see it for yourself the last time you went home?" Xiomara asked. She looked shocked. She wanted information, safety, security.

"No," I said.

I adjusted my purse and looked up to see if I knew anyone in the gallery ahead of us. It was the only place where anything was happening for girls that night. A group was smoking outside a small Technicolor building with DIY painted along the front.

"Let's call Ash right now," Hazel said, exhaling a hit of her spliff. "Get her to answer our questions."

"Don't make her do that," Xiomara said.

I stared at the sidewalk. I threw my Diet Coke bottle in a recycling bin surrounded by dandelions and cigarette butts.

"How did she even get the money to start a commune?" Hazel asked.

The commune started after Ash's mom died and left her their farm. Her mom was so proud of her. The prodigy. The math wiz. I knew Ash sent her mom an insane amount of money. Lucky mom, I thought. When she got sick, dutiful daughter Ash went back home, fixed it up, built extra cabins, and worked remotely. Then after her mom passed away, she invited the lost girls of

Indiana to dance in paradise. It sounded like a wonderland of ketamine, jealousy, nudity, and shooting lessons. Even if it was as different from church as I could imagine, I couldn't shake the memories it brought up of my mom dragging me into the pews. I didn't want to sound too triggered though—or like I didn't love other trans girls—so I'd concealed my fear and delayed visiting. Within the trans-girl community, I always feared the chopping block for my almost heterosexuality. Not that I thought I was oppressed for being straight. I just knew the other girls liked me more when I was potentially fuckable.

"No one can make you do anything," Xiomara said softly. She was probably the only one who knew the full weight of my history with Ash.

"She can. She always can," I whispered. "And anyways, I think I actually want to go."

I tried not to think about the time my conversion therapist told me I was cursed. About the men circling me as they commanded the demons to leave my body. Cult after cult, girl after girl. Their shadows flickered on the walls behind them, taking on winged opaque shapes that oozed pus. My favorite exorcism. My little dance with the devil.

The girls were all looking at me, waiting for me to say something else. To defend my choice. The spliff was nearly out.

"Do we have anything stronger?"

NICE TWINKS

Queens spread below me in crisscrossing sidewalks and power lines. I fumbled my phone out of my tote bag so I could text Nora. We hadn't really ever hung out one-on-one. I didn't imagine our last time together would be quite so charged, but she said she could help me with a getaway car.

At the bottom of the platform, between a Wendy's and an empanada restaurant, Nora was smoking a Virginia Slim. I wanted to get it over with. Get a junky car and speed off. No more gremlins or goblins. They seemed to be growing in number and I wanted to get out of town before their claws ripped me to shreds. If I got out of New York I could get away from all that was haunting me: the slime, the eyes, the snake. All the servants of night. I shuddered walking over to her, blinking a few times to clear the things I saw whenever I closed my eyes. They were bloodshot from the lack of sleep. I was doing way too much ketamine, which only exacerbated the problem. Too much of one potion led me back to another. I'd already downed two coffees that morning before heading to the 7 train. Nora didn't seem to pick up on my mental state though, just nodded at me as I walked up.

"How's it going?" I asked.

"Good," she answered, putting out her cigarette on her thigh highs. She took off her headphones and turned her gaze to me. "My uncle works at this place. I don't know him all that well, but I think we can probably get you a pretty good deal."

"Perfect," I said.

She motioned forward, directing me to the left, as if being chivalrous. I started down the street, dodging people on their way to work. Nora had suggested we go early so we could talk to her uncle alone. I bummed a cigarette off her and took a deep inhale, pressing the thin paper between my lips.

"How's your week going?"

"I had a few gigs, mostly, like, friends of friends' raves. Nothing big."

"What counts as big?"

"Something in Gowanus," she said as she lit another cigarette.

"Is it far?"

She shook her head and inhaled. "No, I just needed another one. I haven't been up this early in a while."

"Were you out late last night?"

"Yeah. Hazel and I partied. Kinda dead but some twink gave us ketamine. He was nice."

"I don't believe in nice twinks," I said.

"Weren't you a twink for a while?"

We stayed quiet as we passed by flower beds and garden gnomes, almost in reverence. It never made sense to me how these still lives we encroached upon could exist so close to underground warehouses and corporate Manhattan spires, but here we all were trying to achieve some idyll.

We made two more stops before reaching the dealership. One for Nora to get a bodega coffee filled to the brim with creamer and another for her to get another pack of cigarettes at the gas station. I wanted another too, craved the thorny hoarseness of a good chain-smoke session. We were still early but I felt the looming threat of defeat.

"There he is," Nora said, pointing her cigarette toward the parade of balloons winding through the lot.

USED USED USED, the front sign scrolled. Toyotas, Hondas, Chevrolets. Some of them I recognized from the men I used to fuck in Indiana. Men loved to tell you the makes and models of their cars while cumming down your throat. In case you forgot who had the power to drive you home.

"Hey," Nora called when we were within earshot.

"Nor-aaaaa," he said, gulping air like a beached whale. His brown-suede suit was stained with jelly. "My favorite li'l niece."

"This is my friend," she said.

"Hello, darling."

I realized immediately that this man was not her uncle. He didn't even look like her. This was trade. Someone would be paying for this car.

"This is a Honda CR-V," he said, pounding a rotund green car with his fist. "Sturdy motherfucker. Could definitely get you somewhere. I could get you this one."

Nora smiled and took another drag.

"No, I need something smaller. Cheaper."

“Mmm, okay, sure. Yeah.”

He started walking and shivered when he heard Nora’s boots clicking behind him. She was so tall. It didn’t make sense why she’d fallen so hard for someone like Hazel.

“This one over here’s a Chevrolet Malibu,” he said, rolling the words like marbles. I nodded disinterestedly. It was better to keep him guessing, at least a little.

“Over here we have a Honda Accord.” He pointed but I saw the price tag before I even let myself look at the whole thing.

“Uncle,” Nora warned.

“There *is* something else I’m practically giving away. It’s a 2003 Honda Civic, kinda beat-up, a little bit rusty. But it runs. And it passed all the basic tests. We can take her for a spin if you’d like.”

Nora pressed my shoulder, pushing me back. “Let me.”

Uncle lit up.

Thirty-five minutes later my savings were gone and I was handing Nora a hamburger from the drive-through. The car smelled musty, and the yellowing upholstery reeked of smoke. It was worth it. Escape was in reach.

“He’s alright,” Nora said before chugging some Mountain Dew and dialing the radio to a classical-music station. “He’s not the best guy I’ve ever met but he obviously comes through. He just needs a little encouragement.”

“I don’t think I’ve fucked a cis guy since Ryan.”

“It’s not so bad,” she said. “They’re just kind of slimy sometimes.”

“Yeah, they’re hard to trust—”

“No, I mean literally.”

While I fished for a fry, the string quartet faded out.

"How did you and Hazel meet?"

"Grindr," Nora answered.

"You're just always so private, like a hot girl behind the curtain. Hazel's like . . . like a whirlwind. You're a little calm for her."

"Isn't that how it always works?" she said. "You find someone who complements you and you go until you can't anymore. Now I just want to settle down. I'm not gonna stop DJing or going out. But it's nice to at least have a home base. Hazel wants to go on and on like an endless open-world RPG."

"Nora."

"Seriously! She wants to feel like nothing she ever does will close a door. So she left me to see what other doors were out there. But I know as well as anyone that Hazel's never going to shut me out completely. At some point she's going to come back."

I'd never heard Nora talk so much, or so openly. Maybe it was because I would be leaving soon, and she didn't have to worry about the repercussions as much. I could tell that she believed in the power of T4T deeply. Most of the girls around me did. Even when they didn't practice it, they held it as something sacred, worthy of aspiring to. We didn't fuck with a lot of the girls who earnestly went after cis men.

"Hazel just wants to have some success before she settles down," Nora said, looking straight ahead as we turned the corner onto her street. Choosing T4T was just choosing one kind of hurt over another. It's no more valiant. It's a survival tactic.

"Yeah," I said. I had no bricks left to build her fantasy, but I could relate.

BAGGAGE

Imagine me in a sleeveless Metallica tee sitting on the hood of my car. No bra. Short shorts. Smoking a Marlboro Red. Ash ate that shit up. It was exactly the right amount of butch. Even before making it out of New Jersey, I'd found the country radio stations and cranked the volume. Honky-tonk angels and vengeful women who threw their men into rivers. By the time I got to Pittsburgh, I was drowning in other women's whiskey tears. Yes, I thought, I have been wronged by cheating no-good dirtbags. A decade earlier, in Indiana, I had listened to songs with the same message but slightly less electric guitar. My mom liked the brand of country songs about shooting men and driving to a new town to start over best. Maybe I could get a gun from Ash.

Hazel was the one who suggested I stop in Pittsburgh. Between our last-hurrah tequila shots and bumps of Nora's cocaine, we talked about the girls who came to and left New York. Few left alive. Some moved to L.A., an even worse fate than death, we teased Hazel. One of the women who left was Greer Lankton, Hazel's hero. After a divorce, a successful but difficult art career, an eating disorder, and a heroin habit, she moved to Chicago to detox. Unfortunately, despite a career comeback, she overdosed at thirty-eight. Her parents (who wanted her to have a sex change so she wouldn't grow up to be a faggot), donated much of her ephemera, documents, and sculptures to a museum in Pittsburgh and washed their hands of her. No one wanted me to be gay or trans or anything. Of course, the ex-husband had created his own competing archive since he owned most of her sculptures. He claimed they were each other's great loves even though in letters she wrote that he'd tried to kill her. The worst thing I can imagine is people who hated me in life trying to profit off me in death. While I was driving out of New York, a man came on the radio to tell me a cis man burned his trans girlfriend alive. A girl is a body to be parked in a lot.

The original archive was enough to warrant a pit stop though. Morbid curiosity about those who came before. It was located in a small redbrick building on an idyllic tree-lined street. The sidewalk gleamed white in the early-afternoon sun. The Andy Warhol Museum was farther south, nearly on the water, looking up at the evergreen cliffs. I could see their peaks in the distance, winding into the raw bluffs of Pennsylvania. It was such a long, rough state. But Ohio was approaching and there I would be able to enter the gray emptiness I was used to.

I stomped my cigarette out by a fire hydrant and knocked on the door, hoping it wasn't the kind of place that required an appointment. A woman in blue greeted me and told me I could look around but officially the museum was closed.

"I'm so sorry," she said. "We'll be open Wednesday."

"Are the archives—can I just take a peek?"

"No, I'm so sorry."

I walked away, dejected. I didn't want to see some local-art bullshit. I wanted to see some dolls and weird letters and self-portraits that led to wormholes. Through the window I saw the woman in blue laughing at something on a computer screen. She couldn't be working that hard.

I wondered if my legacy could fill the back room of a museum in Pittsburgh. Probably not. Maybe Ash would miss me. Maybe my parents would throw a deadname party. Hazel and Xiomara would miss me, for sure. Nora would feel something. I don't know what Ryan would think. He would probably swallow me whole. Write a long caption with florid delicate words like *flaneur*. Men say a lot of things. I'll come back later. When I'm mature. When I'm capable. Love is just so much work. Ryan wanted things to work. I never doubted that. Ash too. I get it. Loving trans girls is hard, even when you are one. Loving us is like reaching into a waterfall and trying to pull. You can't get anywhere like that.

I decided to grab some greasy diner food. One of the few things I missed about Indiana was cheap small-town food. Grits, pancakes, burgers, shakes, and those awful pale fries. Pie too. Some places had really good pie. Maybe I had watched too much *Twin Peaks* and found a strange comfort in dark Americana. I think Ryan wanted to force-femme me into playing Audrey. The weirdest things always made him hard.

"What can I get you?"

I ordered breakfast. Coffee and a veggie omelet. The woman clogged away to the steel counter swathed in orange memorabilia and brown stains. An old man in the booth next to me dribbled something green and gassy from his chin. I could tell a few people were looking at me, trying to place what was off.

"Here, baby," said a woman trying to airplane some applesauce or pureed pumpkin into her child's mouth. A little powder-blue lump in a high chair.

Ash always wanted to be a mother. She was always much more certain than I was. The thought only ever tantalized me. I never fully committed. She was the place I wanted to return to. Before Herculine, Ash had been my lighthouse. I was always waiting to come back to port. In the back of my head, I knew we would find our way back to each other someday. Even while she was still in Oakland, we had phone dates. She wrote me love poems about getting lost in SFMoMA and wishing we could go to Bodega Bay together. She was on a real lost-lesbian-love kick, but I bought in.

Ash started transitioning a few months after we met. We weren't as close before. The rumblings were already there, but I didn't know. Ash didn't seem to either. Her few cis lesbian friends started asking her weird questions, so she ended up spending more and more time in my dorm. We kicked out my roommate and pretended to have sex. We sat on the floor and listened to Fiona Apple, each judging the other's predictable mid-2000s taste. She thought learning pop songs on the guitar was a way to reclaim her femininity in a subversive way. We started walking each other to class, creating shelter in each other's arms. I made her tea when she came out to her parents and waited for her at the bus stop after her first HRT appointment. We went the long way to the feminist bookstore. Sometimes they hosted famous lecturers and offered free wine. No one carded. It was one of the few social events we felt okay going to, though Ash was still a visual curiosity to a lot of people. Commuting was brutal. I watched her eyes flash with rage.

Still, she would say hello to the people staring at her, shaming them into something like humanity.

One night near the end of our sophomore year, Ash kissed me outside that bookstore. She tasted like mint gum, cigarettes, and chardonnay. I kissed her back without thinking.

After that we were together more or less.

Early on, I told Ash that I thought there were two kinds of dates: ones where you talked and ones where you listened. I told her she was the first person I'd dated who was different. She laughed at me and said that was because I was hiding myself until I found someone safe.

"Then you get excited."

She licked her spoon clean with a slow flourish. We were sitting in the parking lot of a big grocery store eating strawberry ice cream.

"I don't want to Manic Pixie Dream Girl anyone . . ."

"Well then don't. It's not that hard." She took my hand in hers and folded her fingers over mine. "I'm just saying, I'm here. I'm right in front of you."

"How Buddhist of you."

"I try."

Junior year was full of mistakes. Over the holidays Ash told me she wasn't ready to meet my mom. Two days before Thanksgiving, I was standing in her driveway, yelling through the screen door. Her roommate glared at me.

"Why not?"

Hot snot and cold feet. I heard an acorn fall a few feet away.

"I just came out to my parents. I don't want to meet someone else's yet," she said between clenched teeth.

She was fighting back tears and talking into her arm. The roommate guided her inside. I got in my car and drove two hours to my mom's without a girlfriend.

"I'm so sorry we didn't get to meet her," my mom said.

My grandma smiled and passed the cranberry sauce she knew I did not want.

I can't blame Ash. I hadn't told my family she was trans.

Sometime after we broke up the first time, I listened to a Buddhist dharma talk on what to do when a member of the sangha causes great harm. Do you cast them out or continue to allow them to come and meditate?

Thinking about Ash still feels like that, alternating between reliving visceral memories and intellectualizing the experience. Letting go and learning to sit with the feeling. It was supposed to make it easier to ignore the highs and lows, though eventually they collapsed into one piercing gold shudder.

In the spring, I started wondering about my gender too. The school counselor and I had started unpacking conversion therapy—barely—and talking about the feelings Ash brought up in me.

"Did you want to be her? Or did you love her?"

"Both," I said. Always both.

Two weeks later I was on the same bus I used to pick up Ash from. There was only one doctor in our college town if you wanted hormones.

Not long before finals Ash and I made up. We agreed we wanted to be friends. As two of the very small number of trannies in our college town, we decided to make a pact. We would keep each other safe. She tried to teach me things at first, which made me uncomfortable—standing next to me in front of the mirror, she told me the best razor to get, which foundation wouldn't make me look like a horse, the easiest way to inject, how to deal with the anger. But her lessons didn't stick. While Ash externalized her anger at anything that moved, I began to bury mine. I followed the path of least resistance.

We both lived alone senior year, which made some things easier and some things harder. I started working at a movie theater, shoveling popcorn and scrolling Grindr at 2:00 a.m. after my shift finally ended. By then I had started to intuit that my journalism degree was going to be useless. I started fucking townies with one-eyed cats and horror-DVD collections.

One of the townies tried to threaten me after sex. He told me I was going to hell as his face twisted into something rabid. I didn't think of it as violent, just creepy. He told me we were both going down for our transgressions. I ran out and drove home. I tried to tell Ash, but the words wouldn't come out right and she seemed to think I was just describing a kind of weird encounter. I didn't use any language that was too alarming I guess. She held me for a few minutes and then said we should go out for a drink.

"I'm gonna stay home," I said.

"Okay," she said, grabbing the keys. In retrospect, she was probably horny.

After that, I stayed even closer to Ash. I was afraid of walking on my own too late at night and struggled to do homework for more than an hour at a time. Ash finished her history degree while taking a few odd coding classes. Every Sunday we grocery shopped at Kroger together. It didn't take long until she made a move. We were watching the New Year's ball drop and Mariah Carey's failed lip sync. She leaned over and kissed me with chocolate and almonds stuck in her teeth.

We blissfully shacked up for the rest of the year—almost. There was one week we spent apart after I told her one of the townies I'd slept with had asked to hang out again. She simply couldn't compute that anything had happened to me while we weren't together.

On the last day of classes, Ash offered me a smooshed PB&J from her bag.

"I'm not taking your PB&J. You need to eat," I said.

"So do you."

"Fuck, we're late," I said, shoving the dry bread in my mouth. "Okay, let's go."

"I love you."

"I love you too."

When she moved to Oakland she started posting inspirational quotes underneath her selfies. Sometimes they sounded like poems. It was very Female Small Business Owner (Trans Edition)™. I worked at a fast-food chain in our college town and saved up to move to New York. I wanted to work at one of those failing feminist news websites specializing in enlightened clickbait. I pitched them a story about losing my virginity in the woods and never heard back.

In New York, I started again. We decided after a few months of long distance that it would be better for both of us to live our lives separately and make new connections. I decided to be a slut. I fucked any cis guy who messaged me back. It took a year to get it out of my system, before I met Hazel and Xiomara and started fucking Ryan.

Eventually Ash called and asked me if I would be on her care team.

"What?"

"I'm getting a pussy, bitch!"

We screamed and screamed. I was so happy for her. I was so happy I would get to see her again.

I refused to look God in the face as the plane touched down. The whole ride my stomach kept flipping. The only movie they were showing on the coast-to-coast flight was *When Harry Met Sally . . .*

It was my first time on the West Coast and Ash wanted me to remember everything. It was easy to love, at the time—the azure sky, the beauty of optimistic green-juice devotees, the pink sea.

I took her to a diner, my treat. It was a bit of a joke since she hated diner food. Our waiter kept hovering nearby anxiously. It was probably clear to everyone around us that we were about to have a "talk." Neither of us had said a word in a while, sipping our coffees quietly. Ash was wearing a pink crop top and jeans. I'd made a myth out of her and then there she was again, as willowy and wispy as ever. She seemed older too, a little less eager.

In the year plus after our breakup I'd tried to be more cautious. Only sex, no emotions. I knew from the internet that she'd had a string of lovers, but during our weekly phone calls she never mentioned anyone.

The waiter came over to take our order. I got grilled cheese with tomato and a side of mayo. Ash laughed and ordered a patty melt.

"At least get a milkshake, bitch," Ash said, eyeing the other people sitting in the restaurant. She kept shifting. A woman in leopard leggings walked in with a newborn. Two older women walked in behind her carrying an assortment of bottles, bibs, and blankets. It seemed like mothers were always walking into diners to remind you who gets to eat peach pie in peace.

"Do you think I would make a good mom?" Ash asked.

"Of course."

"I want kids."

We waited a few minutes for our food, but it didn't come. No mountain of fries or valley of ketchup to distract us.

"Do you really think so?"

Since we'd never lived together, even when we were in the same town, our lives were always constructed in imaginary houses. I didn't get around to telling her what I wanted my house to look like, but Ash painted a beautiful picture of hers: a farmhouse with two daughters, one son, a dog, and a white cat. She even had their names picked out. I caught a glimpse of our possible future then. But she seemed to think my heart wasn't in it, so I deflected, and we moved on to talking about the food.

Driving home, the lights on the hills looked like fireflies. I said as much to her thinking it would sound sweet.

"There aren't any fireflies on the West Coast actually," she corrected, before moving on to dissect the art exhibit we'd seen earlier that day.

"Oh," I said.

I looked it up later. It's not true about fireflies. They're on both coasts, though in the West they don't glow.

I spent a week and a half with her after the surgery. I met a lot of raver girls and admirers, but still couldn't get a sense of what Ash's life on the coast was really like. I had to get back to New York and pay rent. Her best friend in Oakland, Shireen, was going to take the next shift.

"Alright, my love, I have to get to the airport," I said looking down at the dozing dilettante.

"Okay, baby, come down here to my level."

I leaned down to her like Prince Charming waking Snow White, and she jerked up to kiss me and smiled. We stared into each other's eyes for a moment, neither of us knowing that we wouldn't see the other again for a few years. Neither of us knowing much at all except that love was a monument to something holy.

I left Ash to finish her pussy healing, suppressing tears until I got past security. After I got through the pat down, I bawled in front of a water fountain for twenty minutes. No one tried to talk to me. Maybe that was just the West Coast–airport vibe. No one was doing anything that made any sense. I considered going to the airport bar to drink some overpriced wine but decided against it. I tried to sit and read for a while but couldn't make any headway. Flicking through the pictures I'd taken that week, I tried to decide if I should post any. I thought about finally getting a cat.

Eventually I decided to get some coffee to keep myself awake during the flight. I would wait and decide what to do when I was seated between worlds. Airports were sliding doors, but airplanes housed the real oblivion.

The nearest café kiosk was manned by a woman with blue hair. She was scrolling her phone, muttering about an ex. I fell in love with her instantly.

"Can I have a coffee?"

"Anything else?"

"No."

"Men suck," she said, turning her left wrist in circles as she poured the mud-like substance into a plastic cup. I already knew it would burn my hands.

I nodded. "Yeah."

"Don't get a boyfriend."

"I can't say when I date women I have any better luck."

She grinned and laughed, wagging her finger at me. "Ya know, you're right."

I walked back, sat down with my coffee, and watched my hands turn crimson from the heat. If my life were more romantic, I would've looked up and seen Ash. But I didn't. I looked up and instead saw the line to board my flight starting to form.

I fell asleep on the plane and didn't have any dreams, which surprised me. No demons, no hallucinatory hookups. For a long time I had the wildest dreams. I would find myself at Coney Island, King's Cross, the Golden Gate Bridge, places I'd never been. A pack of dogs ran through these settings, leaving clumps of fur behind them.

PART 2

WALK ON YOUR KNEES

I arrived at Herculine at 3:00 p.m. on a Tuesday. Farm animals came into view one by one in all of Noah's zoological splendor. A lone sheep bleated as I slowed down and parked near the main drag of cabins. There were sixteen in all, surrounding a firepit and a big white hall that looked suspiciously like a church. Like the Garden of Eden with mighty oak trees sprouting between the buildings. We were a long way from heaven now. Ash's mom's house was nearly unrecognizable. She had remade it into a sapphic temple. Trans girls milled between the cabins. I took a long breath, amazed at what Ash had accomplished.

As I turned the key out of the ignition, a few girls ambled over to check on me, dragging their feet over the wildflowers. My Civic had gotten me here in one piece. Driving in, I'd had to wind through the limestone, cozying next to steep inclines and descending lower and lower until there were no more vistas to look at.

I got out and stretched my legs, sore after sleeping in a T.J.Maxx parking lot the night before. The cool Indiana breeze fluttered across my face and the afternoon sun broke through the shedding trees like a kind neighbor. All across the land, crimson and dun leaves were already aflame. Fall was coming.

One of the girls wandered closer to me as I pulled my hair back into a ponytail. I was still wearing my Metallica tee even though it was rank. I'd change as soon as I could freshen up. I hoped they had showers. I hoped Ash would take me back in her bed.

"Hey there," the girl said. She was taller than me. Muscular and clad in all black. Her hair was dyed silver, her dark roots sprouting unevenly. She seemed like a regular goth girl without the accessories. "I'm Mira."

She reached out her hand to me like a welcome fairy. I'd never heard Ash mention her before but recognized her from social media. I realized Ash almost never used the girls' names, so I'd referred to them in my head using only abstract signifiers: the Hot Butch, the One with Pink Hair, the Girl with the Septum Piercing.

"I'm looking for Ash," I said after introductions. "She's expecting me."

"I know," Mira said with a smile. "Follow me."

We walked past a few of the cabins. They were well-made, not cheap bullshit. Ash must've hired people to help. Or maybe one of the butches was a carpenter in a past life. Carpentry was one of the hottest professions. I loved imagining what carpenters could do with their hands.

"You know all about Herculine then?" Mira asked.

"I do. I remember when Ash first told me she was going to build a commune. We grew up together."

"She really helped me. I was in a conversion therapy program for a few weeks before she got me out."

Ash had not told me about any rescue operations. I looked at Mira, trying to see through the cool darkness of her eyes. She didn't give me anything, just ushered me along through the camp. The main hall loomed before us, the river that divided the encampment just beyond. A few more girls walked around near the fence. I couldn't see the sheep anymore, but the air still smelled like dung. I noticed a few bluebells sprouting from the sheep shit. In the distance, a single cow stared vacantly ahead, frozen in time. I wondered if the girls knew how to take care of animals. I certainly didn't.

"We have a cow, a sheep, and a few pigs, but we're trying to buy more," Mira explained, catching my gaze. "Ash should be in here or her study. It's the oldest building besides her house, the first thing she built when she got the land from her mom."

She smiled like a tour guide.

"Okay," I said.

"Go on in," Mira said.

I took a step inside and closed the heavy door behind me. I didn't want our reunion to be on display. The main hall felt like a fun house, a combo library/chapel filled with white benches decorated with carvings of Indiana flora and fauna—white-tailed deer, bobcats, a depressed-looking barn owl. Ash wasn't usually so patriotic. I stopped to finger the outline of a cardinal. The benches faced a ghoulish effigy wearing a hazmat suit that was surrounded by decaying lilies. Ash would have an explanation. It was probably some renowned trans-woman plague doctor or something. Still, I resolved to stay on the other side of the room while I waited for her.

The walls were lined with old oak bookshelves that looked like they were about to fall. I peered at the moldy science fiction paperbacks and kabbalah texts and found a history of cannibalism next to a coloring book. Odd. I was still wary of the permeable boundary between commune and cult and the reading list was certainly not helping. I felt moved to pray. It seemed like the thing to do in such a space. The only time I still tried was when something demonic was stalking me. Which, to be fair, had become fairly frequent.

I realized I hadn't told my friends that I'd arrived. They renamed the group chat LESBIAN U-HAUL ACCOUNTABILITY before I left and specifically instructed me to send along Herculine updates. In movies about trans women, we always exist in isolation. The Trans-Girl Actress always stood alone, waiting for a chaser or to be berated. They never had group chats with their friends where they shared little jokes and memes and voice notes and rants. My phone didn't have service, but I was sure I'd be able to get on the Wi-Fi soon. So far it seemed like a self-sufficient community. Ash had done it. A place by girls for girls. I reread the last few texts I'd sent the group.

made it through Pittsburgh !!
greer lankton archives were closed

fuck ohio

Xiomara: [laughing emoji]

Hazel: did u make it there yet??

Xiomara: u good? are u already fucking?

I walked to the center of the room and took a deep breath, feeling like I was on the precipice of something. Boot steps sounded outside as a shadow crossed the chapel. She stood in the doorway. We were alone again. In the stray scratches of afternoon light, Ash's hands were stained a pale green and caked in dirt. A yellow wildflower peeked out of her short brown hair. It looked like a last-minute addition. She wore black shorts and a grass-stained white tank that showed off all her tattoos and bulging muscles. I wondered when she got jacked. I hadn't noticed in pictures.

I shuddered. A cool current coursed through my body. Nothing had prepared me for her presence. I wanted to grab her, kiss her, and hold her against my body but something stopped me. We stared at one another, waiting, each taking in the shock of the other. My eyes flashed a message to her. Something hot spread across my pussy. She felt it and walked over to me, wordless, grinning. I was silent as her hands grazed my back. I wanted her body to hit me like a wave, but she was drawing out the inevitable surf. I wanted her to slap me, to break me out of the last anxious week, to redeem me through pain. Give us this day our daily bread.

Ash looked uncertain for a moment, her eyes like two swirling whirlpools. Then her pupils dilated, and everything was exactly like before. She coordinated every move, dragging my hair with her muddy hands. My body fell with a thud under hers as she reached inside and fucked me. How many words do I know? None when I'm being fucked open. I trembled with gasps of exploration. When I reached out to touch her tits, she swatted my hand away and pinned me to the floor. She went down on me and scratched my thigh with one of her nails. In a single motion she began sucking the blood from my wound—not that there was much at first, but she drew more after she bit down. I wasn't unused to a casual hickey, but I cried out from the pain. Her fingers wormed back into me, and she started to lick my thigh a little wolfishly. I was being marked. No one else would touch me after this.

"What do you want?" Ash asked, pumping me with a few fingers and letting her other hand rest on my pre-op pussy. I laughed. She slapped me. Across the face, open palm. My face stung but mostly from surprise. "What do you want?"

When our eyes met again, I couldn't place her empty look. It wasn't shared history, it was something feral. The wild hookup I'd imagined in my head was just the beginning of some long maze Ash was navigating. This was what she wanted, a power-up. She put her fingers into my mouth and leaned over me. The floor was starting to feel hard against my back. Lust didn't overcome all. Ash's hands tasted like dirt, and still I worried I smelled foul.

As she her dangled fingers in my mouth, pressing nail against tooth, thumb against gum, she said, "Tell me what you want."

"Whip me," I answered.

Easy corporal punishment. Pain was even better than sex sometimes. It reminded me of my body's limits. Targeted pain was the opposite of dissociation. Stay—with—the—pain, my brain yelled. Thich Nhat Hanh would be proud. If Ash hadn't seemed so in character I would've made the joke aloud.

"Walk on your knees," Ash commanded.

She walked past the effigy and opened a small closet full of toys. Many of them I recognized from the time I took care of her. Meanwhile, I was trying to crawl like a sexy, virginal nymph. Ash almost rolled her eyes and walked back over to me.

"Off," she commanded. I slipped off my tee and she whipped my bare back without warning.

"One," she counted. "You have until five to get to the front of the room. And I didn't say crawl, did I?"

I rose onto my knees and tried to figure out how to properly follow her instruction. Ash gave me just enough time and humility to make it to her.

"You made me wait so long," she said.

We weren't just talking about sex anymore. I could feel how wet I was getting. Tech money often made people bad tops, but Ash was the exception, she knew what she was doing. The last time we had sex I was left with welts for weeks. It wasn't the kind of thing Ryan or any of the boys I saw in New York could accomplish.

"Please," I simpered.

"Please what, babe? Harder?" She let the whip gently caress my back. "Tell me what you want. I missed you."

I could tell she was almost about to cry. I didn't want that; she got mean when she cried. Weakness didn't suit her just like power never suited me.

"Please fuck me," I said.

She slowly flipped me over, so I was on my back, and crawled on top of me, her mouth wide and hair falling in ringlets above my face.

"You were gone for so long, my love."

"I'm here, aren't I?" I responded, panting hard as she closed one hand under me and dug around with the other to find an opening.

I forgot how good she was at muffing. But, of course, Ash had practice. After a while she clawed my head between her legs and let me eat her out. I could have listened to her squeak all day, but she flipped me over again, forcing me up against the effigy as she went four fingers in. I came hard imagining sleeping next to her later that night.

We both wanted to roost with each other in a cozy little nest when all else fell apart. To sneak past the ruptures in our lives. I swear I wanted to be happy. I swear I thought I was going in the right direction.

HONEYSUCKLE

After sex, we had more sex. Then Ash took me to her cabin. We did more of the same. Less blood, more passion.

"Dinnertime," she said after her third orgasm. I didn't even have time to take stock of her belongings.

For a lesbian commune, the girls read surprisingly little Sylvia Plath. There was, however, a large number of girls with dyed hair. A few girls went natural, a nod to the hippiedom of a bygone era. None of the girls were faithless. All believed in something. Tarot, Buddhist self-help, Mary Oliver tattoos, T4T, signed books by the big trans-girl authors. The group was made up almost entirely of white trans girls. A few came from white trash trailer parks, but most were still getting used to roughing it.

Ash hadn't yet shown me the cabins, but I assumed from her hands around my waist that I was going to be staying with her. A little concubine for the queen. I was flattered. Lay claim to me, I thought, knowing full well that was what she'd always wanted to do. She'd gotten me to move, to give in to her. I didn't know if I felt good about it but couldn't persuade myself otherwise either. I just knew she was the love of my life even if it didn't look the same way to me as it did to her. She wanted a co-ruler, an empire, to be a trans mom to the masses. I wanted a little picket fence and the ability to say hi to my neighbor. Unfortunately conservative. But Ash had a plan, and I didn't. It was good enough for now.

I looked down at the soft green-and-pink blobs floating in my bowl. The cook's name was Natalie, a bright twiggy girl. She was about twenty-three, five months on hormones, and had been a line cook in Fort Wayne for years before that. I tried to avoid her as she was a little too chatty and overly familiar. None of the other girls seemed to like her either. When she finally sat down to eat, no one moved over to make room for her. She ate at the end of the bench gesticulating wildly to herself.

"Martha! Sit by me," she squealed. A tired-looking girl with a septum piercing, white crop top, and tattooed torso walked over. Martha started nodding along as Natalie animatedly launched into an account of her day in the kitchen.

Most of the food was brought in from a town a few miles away. Ash raised money every way she knew how. Some of the girls cammed, some scammed Amazon, everyone chipped in farming. A GoFundMe generated a small amount of money for the group. Natalie sold things at the farmers market, though apparently people weren't so welcoming there. And Mira, whom I'd met earlier, had recently sold a few feet pics to a guy in Russia who she thought might be a serious hacker. She'd laid a trap and blackmailed some cash out of him before he disappeared.

"He was so scared when I told him I had his wife on speed dial. I actually did. I sent him his wife's number and a picture of her I found online." Mira laughed, her silver hair swishing around. I'd learned that when she first arrived at Herculine, Ash told her she couldn't dye her hair green anymore, it was too on the nose.

One time Mira got a big grocery shipment "accidentally" delivered to the group. They all ate Ben & Jerry's for a month. Each girl's popularity was determined by a matrix of skill, likability, and fuckability. They flitted around in a haze of tits and ass and tattoos as I plotted their positions in the lesbian web of hookups and breakups.

Martha, the Girl with a Septum Piercing, handled finances. She collected money from the girls who could bring it in, helped them find side hustles for the greater good, and tried to keep the peace about how much each could keep for herself. Indigo seemed to take care of all other business. The scraggly butch had joined the project early on after surviving electroshock therapy in Elkhart. She knew her way around animals. Pigs, cows, deer. Roasting, tracking, hunting. Occasionally she walked around with a bow and arrow, making everyone else uncomfortable. She even buzzed her own hair.

"She's a Taurus," Mira whispered to me, as if that explained it. Indigo did not sit at our table.

Herculine still seemed to be running on a shoestring budget mostly funded by Ash. She had kept her tech job and added on a consulting gig, starting work at five in the morning so she could spend most of the afternoon and evening helping the girls. I noted her schedule closely. Before they had reliable internet access, Ash had to drive around to find Wi-Fi.

"I met a lot of John Waters characters that way. People who would let me work at their places if I sucked their toes, broke their knees, shit like that," she explained.

But eventually Ash got power, literally. Electricity, I discovered, was tightly monitored. Ash had forced the local municipal utility to plug her into the power grid and bought plenty of backup generators just in case. Running water proved more elusive, though she had triumphed there as well after a few years and some plumbing accidents. I was coming in at the end of their industrial revolution. Money was tight but scarcity was no longer something that drove the girls to hunger.

"But everyone's so generous," Martha said, spilling her stew as she spoke. "You're going to fit right in."

I was the twentieth girl to join Herculine. No one talked about me like I was a temporary addition. Maybe Ash had forgotten to tell them I wasn't committing for life, just trying it on for size. When I looked up from my bowl, I caught Mira smiling blankly at me, but she barely registered my discomfort. In fact, any time I turned around, I noticed another girl staring and smiling at me like a marionette. One sitting across from me had seemingly appeared out of nowhere. Her mouth was moving silently, tongue curling out vowels and consonants as if reciting an incantation. Maybe she worshipped Mother Gaia or something, one of the hippie elect concentrating on getting closer to nature. I turned away from her and toward my food. When I looked back up, the girl was gone. No one else seemed to notice.

"Did you see that girl?" I asked Mira.

"Which one?" She laughed.

"I don't know. Never mind."

Most days, they sat at these picnic tables across from the mess hall, until it got too cold. The first winter was apparently pretty brutal. I don't remember Ash talking about it much on the phone. Some years she just hadn't called as much. The last year or so was when she became really insistent on bringing me out, but even before we always joked about West Coast versus East Coast. Longing was easier than reunion. We both traced the other's absence and imagined her always doing the right thing.

Now, in person, I remembered how charismatic she was, how easily she could turn her presence off and on. Back in Oakland, she had no problem making friends. Everywhere she went it seemed like people wanted to talk to her. Rich cis men, old lesbians at the farmers market, other trans girls just starting hormones. It made sense she'd want to utilize that charisma for something more organized.

"She rescued us," a young girl in a baby doll dress told me. Jesus, I thought, hardly any of these girls were over twenty-three.

"I think most? All?" The girl's voice kept climbing up an octave. "A lot of us were in conversion therapy before. But then we climbed onto Ash's motorcycle and got hormones and shit. She steals them."

"You ride a motorcycle now?" I asked, whirling around like a jealous lover to face Ash. I was practically straddling her.

"Yeah. I got my license while I was taking care of my mom."

"Jesus Christ," I said.

"What?"

"You never told me. I want to ride on a motorcycle."

"You never have?"

The other girls were watching our tennis match. I wasn't trying to compete. I'd known Ash forever. But clearly I'd stepped into something even though I hadn't meant to.

"No," I said quietly.

"You have to take her, Ash. You have to take her! It's so much fun," the girl in the baby doll dress panted.

All I could see from the back of Ash's motorcycle were her broad shoulders. Wind bled my face dry as we sped through the evergreens. My fingernails etched marks into her sides. Earlier she'd put on my helmet and smirked like I didn't know what I was doing. She was right. No hot-girl motorcycle rides for me. It was always just a fantasy. I'd seen the trans women speeding around in Brooklyn, the pictures of Kathy Acker. I'd always wanted to do something useful with my body like that. Bodybuilding, dancing, anything besides walking and lying on my back.

We turned abruptly onto a dirt road once we were a few miles away from Herculine. It looked like a generic nature preserve with a gravel parking lot. Dusk was clearing the oak trees. Indiana nights were so still. Movement always seemed peripheral, a few cars, the threat of cops, but usually any noise ended up belonging to a raccoon or a squirrel, sometimes a deer or an owl. Not Bigfoot. Ash chained her bike to a wooden post and started down the dusty path, overgrown with threads of clover.

"I feel like I missed so much," I said. The sweet smell of sweat was radiating off my body like poison. I hadn't changed since arriving. My Metallica tee was soaked with cum and fast-food grease.

"You did, but I don't know, sometimes it seems like memory doesn't work that way. Like when I see you no time has passed. I forget you were ever somewhere else. Do you think you'll miss New York?"

"I'll go back eventually," I said.

"I never really miss Oakland, to be honest," Ash said, ignoring me and chewing on her own intellectual worms. "I never felt rooted. It was nice when you were there though. When I came back and started taking care of my mom I felt like everything came into focus for me. I knew what I wanted."

I wondered how many times she had given this speech.

"Do you miss your mom?" I asked. I felt a little guilty since I hadn't gone back for the funeral. Getting off work was impossible, and my own mom ate the little time I did have, demanding my presence over the holidays.

"Of course," Ash said. "My mom was pretty good to me, to be honest. She really believed in this."

Neither of us had grown up poor. My mom was nice and generous, but she never paid my rent or anything like that. I was the one who chose to suffer in the city. I didn't have anything to complain about. I just didn't seem to have what Nora or the Hot Freelance Girls or the Trans-Girl Actress had. I wondered how Ash handled different girls' expectations for a certain amount of luxury in the commune.

We stopped at a clearing and lay down. I didn't want to spoil the mood by expressing my doubts. Eventually I would have to puncture Ash's fantasy about the two of us being some sort of royal utopian couple but not yet. Selfishly I wanted the romance to play out first. I needed to buy myself time, figure some things out. I wasn't sure precisely what. Trauma? That's not very answerable. Good politics can't fix you. Good intentions won't save you.

Surrounded by honeysuckle, Ash looked like a princess. For a moment, her hard halo cracked, leaving a tired woman behind. I hoped she could still get us home without crashing.

"Do you remember the time we got so high after the election?" I asked.

"Yes." She snorted.

"I didn't think the exit ramp would hold us down. I couldn't figure out how gravity worked."

"You're always trying to get as low to the ground as you can."

We were silent as I watched a crow land on top of a tree stump. It was a tiny thing, probably just out of the nest. Cicadas conducted a symphony in B-flat.

"You did it," I said finally. "You made a family."

"Yeah, well. You came a few years in."

"You didn't tell me how hard it was at first."

"I didn't want to worry you. And I really didn't want you to tell me to quit."

"I would have."

Ash laughed. The big kind of laugh we used to share on nights out in college.

"Yeah, you want safety. I still can't promise that. We do a lot of shit to get by but it's still hard. Getting power and stuff was a big win though. I wish we were fully self-sufficient so I could quit my job but it's just not realistic."

"You're doing a great job, babe."

"I hope so."

She started crawling over the honeysuckle toward me, letting the yellow crunch beneath her. I loved feeling the grass cut against my bare legs.

"You have such a beautiful smile," Ash whispered. "I wish I could kiss you to some stupid country song inside a stupid bar."

"Tequila kisses."

She nodded. Her eyes dilated again, just as they had right before she kissed me in the meeting hall.

"You wanted this, right?"

"I did," I said, before pausing. "I do."

"Good. You can help."

A lump formed in my throat like a stone frog.

"I don't think I have a lot to offer."

"You'll still have to put some work in, babe. Even if you're mine."

I flinched but tried to play it off like simmering desire. I kissed her with my open mouth, trying to douse the doubt. The best lie is the one you convince yourself is true.

"I missed you," I said. It was true. I'd always wanted to come back and find Ash to test our love. I just never measured the quicksand gulf between desire and commitment.

"I missed you too, honeysuckle."

GREAT WORK OPPORTUNITY

I woke up and found all the sheets on the floor. Ash was still dozing lightly next to me. I took a picture of the two of us and sent it to the group chat and wrote "u-hauling" under it. I looked at my small tits and hugged them to my body. The sunrise was still gathering heat. Her room was full of neat walnut furniture. Nothing seemed out of place. No more posters, no TV, no pile of laundry. Gauzy white curtains and the canopy above her bed fluttered against the gray morning light. A vase full of wildflowers stood on her dresser next to a bag of ketamine. I opened a drawer and pulled out a white tank. My own luggage was tucked under the bed, still untouched and neatly packed. I wanted to smell like Ash. I was okay with ownership when it served me.

I knew I had to call my mom. We didn't check in every day, but I tried to maintain a good relationship. Going no contact was never remotely within the realm of possibility. I loved her even if there were untouched minefields in our past. I was always glad when I called and there weren't any major holidays on the horizon. Those required more negotiation. I had told her I was going to crash with Ash, who she knew in broad strokes, but left the rest vague. I pitched it as a "great work opportunity." Before I called my mom I checked back in with the girls. Signal was still spotty, but I tried to make the most of it.

Xiomara: i'm glad u made it there
okay, what's it like?

it's okay, we're still fucking
a lot. trying to adjust. kinda
weird

Hazel: omg yay. get it. i leave for
L.A. tomorrow

Nora: wear a condom

When I finally called my mom, she had a lot of questions. I did too.

"So you're at a camp?"

"I don't think you ever met my friend Ash but she started a sort of . . . group."

"A group?" she repeated, looping the vowels. Her egg timer went off in the background. The Doberman barked. "And what are you doing there?"

"I'm reconnecting with an old friend," I said.

"And working?"

"Ash works at a tech company and offered to train me."

"Doing what? Coding?"

"Kind of," I said. "And some other stuff. Design, networking, that kind of thing."

"Look, I mean, you're twenty-six so you can do whatever you want."

"I know."

"But at some point you have to start . . . making it work," she said. I wasn't sure what *it* was. Life?

"I am, I am making it work. This will be good."

"Okay. Just be careful out there. If something goes wrong just come up here, alright?" She took a bite of something crunchy, spitting over the static. "I have to head to the ER in a few. Are you gonna be safe out there?"

"Yeah, Mom, I'm fine. I've known Ash a long time. She's a good person."

"That's what I thought about your dad." She laughed. "But I'm sure you're right. Call me soon?"

My mom was close with her dad, but I was closer with her mother. She was the one who taught me how to pray, one of the few people I could always find some kind of refuge in, even if we disagreed about a lot of things. Every so often we went to the hibachi grill downtown, always just the two of us because my mom and grandpa didn't like it. They stayed at home and ordered pizza or ate leftovers. My grandma took me to antique shops, drank Folgers coffee, and loved diners. That was probably where I got it from. When I slept over, we stayed up late watching the *Twilight Zone* and *I Love Lucy* marathons. She made me listen to the Beach Boys and Frank Sinatra until I knew every word. I was devastated when she died.

One time when my grandma and I went out for hibachi, she ordered sake. She told me how lonely she was after my grandpa died. Apparently, another man at her church was trying to court her but she couldn't do it, even though he was "very sexy." She never said things like that sober. I never saw her drink again.

Grandma did seem to like independent women. My mom took after her that way. Unfortunately, I was neither independent nor married. Not that it mattered, I wasn't part of our biological woman lineage. My mom never talked to me or thought of me that way. She only told me about the things I'd inherited from my dad.

"He was very artistic," my mom said, making it sound like a slur.

When I got off the phone, I decided to stretch my legs and continue to build out my mental map of the place. Not that it was so hard to wrap my head around its layout. All the cabins faced toward the chapel Ash and I had fucked in. I quickly checked on my car to make sure it was still standing. It was. No dents or scrapes.

There were girls everywhere I went. Mira and the girl in the baby doll dress—now wearing a white sundress and a few jangly bracelets—were coming back from a trip to the store. I realized I didn't know who could pass in rural Indiana. They probably sent the less vulnerable girls. Mira grabbed a bunch of supermarket bags and left the two of us standing alone.

"Hi—" I couldn't remember her name.

"Elle," she cooed. Elle oozed innocence, as if unscarred by her past or the future that awaited her. I knew I could just as easily have been misjudging her because of the baby aesthetic. Maybe, like everything else, it was a trauma response. "How was your motorcycle ride last night?"

"Good," I said simply.

"Elle and I were just talking about dinner last night," Mira said after she returned.

"What about it?" I asked.

"We thought Natalie was being soooo annoying."

"What'd she do?"

"You didn't see her practically cornering Martha? That girl's too horny for her own good. I want to like her but . . ."

I couldn't keep the girls straight. They were like Ash's minions, carefully poised like little dolls with painted-on smiles.

"Mira!" Elle interjected. "Play nice."

"I didn't notice," I said.

"You were distracted," Mira said. Elle laughed. "Practically crawling in Ash's lap. Some people won't be too happy about that."

"We've known each other a long time." I blushed. They both smirked. "Is everyone here so young?"

"I think Ash and Indigo are the oldest."

They started mumbling among themselves.

"Do you two smoke?" I tried.

"I don't," Elle said.

"Oh."

"It's so bad, with the estrogen and all."

"Well, yeah."

Mira offered me a half-hearted smile as if to apologize for Elle and we parted ways. Elle waved me off with the warmest expression. I watched Martha walk by a few minutes later. She waved at me too. I bit my lip and put my hands in my pocket. Natalie followed a little later, trying to be inconspicuous.

I lit up a cigarette by the little river and put my legs in. Ash would find me soon, accept my gift, and put me to work—but for a moment I turned my head to the sky and let my legs soak. Squishy green muck collected between my toes. While I was wondering if they rationed coffee, I saw Indigo walking toward the woods. The hills all around the commune were thick with trees. She was grimly plodding away from the camp toward the tallest peak. I realized it was probably a good vantage from which to survey the whole commune. I decided to follow her. She was wearing a white muscle tee and camo pants. Ash was one of the few women I'd ever dated, but Indigo would've been my type if she didn't so clearly hate me. I didn't tell Ash. I was too new to know what subterranean alliances existed beyond my intuition.

A few days in, it was clear that the girls were hiding something from me. I would walk into a room or stumble upon two of them whispering and they'd abruptly stop and stare blankly at me before cracking a smile. Maybe they were having money problems. Or they were doing something illegal to fund the operation and didn't want to tell me about it just yet. I was being too suspicious. Not everything was a racket. Trans-girl utopia had to exist somewhere. If not New York, why not Indiana? I could learn to be a good wife to Ash. I could wash her clothes and cook for her. I could teach a girl a few months on E how to love her changing body, walk her to the river and baptize her in self-acceptance. Teach her the fallacies of common first-year trans-girl mistakes. Of course, all the times Ash had broken me before weren't far from my mind. But I'd always imagined we would find our way back to each other.

A murder of crows scattered in the distance. I'd noticed that the fauna around us seemed oddly quiet. As their midnight-colored wings beat, they made no noise, cresting silently into the pale-blue sky. I didn't know what to make of it. Indigo wasn't too far ahead of me. Birches and oaks flanked the beginning of the path, so it was easy to follow along. We were winding deeper into the woods now, farther away from Herculine. I wondered if I would be able to find my way home.

The leaves crackled underneath my crusty tennis shoes. Beasts and spirits could hide all around me in crevices, under boulders, in fox holes. I shivered just thinking about it. No more visions, I told myself. No more fear. But even as I thought it, the miasma constricted around my heart. Paranoia does not let the neurotic rest, even after escaping a city full of dead ends.

"Are you even trying?" Indigo turned toward me with a blank face, her bow swung across her shoulder. She was a few hundred feet ahead of me, paused in a clearing.

"No," I said. I hadn't decided on how secretive I was trying to be. Mainly I was following a hunch. I needed to learn as much as I could about the power dynamics of the camp. I hadn't considered how much noise I could make—rocks slid, twigs creaked, gravel shifted. "I guess not."

"Have you ever gone hunting?"

"No. My mom always wanted to teach me how to shoot but never did."

"If a bunch of trans girls were using guns in the middle of the woods we'd be killed. That's why I hunt this way."

"Do you still need a license?" I mumbled.

We mounted a small knoll surrounded by prickly weeds.

"If you're going to come with me, you're going to have to shut the fuck up," Indigo said. "Your feet too."

"Shut my feet up?"

Indigo started walking away. Quietly, I noticed.

"You're so stupid," she said.

"Fuck off."

I started back toward the camp, but she was standing in front of me before I could register how she'd moved so fast.

"Move," I tried to say, but the word sounded like piss in my mouth.

"She's not like she was," Indigo said. Up close I saw she wore a dainty silver cross necklace around her neck. She was covered in bruises.

"I'm not either."

"Enjoy it while it lasts," she said.

"What do you mean?" I asked.

"If you think she loves you and you're going to have an easy time here . . ."

"I don't think that."

Maybe I did. But I wasn't going to let a bitch think I was simple.

"You're going to get yourself kicked out if you're not careful," she said. She lifted one of her boots and smoothed a patch of silt.

"Stop with the cryptic wisdom and just beat me up if that's what you want."

"I'm not playing some sort of psychosexual game. I'm not her."

"Why won't you say her name?"

Indigo started walking out of the clearing toward the tree line.

"You won't be the favorite for long. You're too much of a smart-ass. She likes girls who don't ask questions."

"Who do you think she prefers? Some little wood nymph two months on E?"

She laughed at me. A real laugh, cutting and brisk like the wind had been knocked out of her.

"Love the solidarity. I'm sure you're gonna make a great impression and no one's going to start secretly hating you."

"I know how to deal with that," I said.

"You don't know what it's like here." Her voice was low and sandpapery. She really was pulling off her whole thing. "We have twenty girls here now, *honeysuckle*." I bucked, bracing for an oncoming icy dissociation head rush that wouldn't clear.

"And you're telling me what? They were Ash's and she tossed them out when she got tired of them?"

"Whatever you think you can give her, I've already given her. And better. I bet you don't even top." Indigo smiled wickedly.

"Shut up," I said.

"You should get out of here. You don't know what Ash is really like."

"I've known her longer than you."

"Not like I have," she said as she quickly walked away, leaving me alone in the woods. I crossed hunting off my great-work-opportunities list.

SHADOWBOXING

The rest of my first week passed sweetly. I began the long task of catching up Ash on my life and she offered salacious details about the commune in return. We lay under her gauzy canopy bed listening to the early-light birdcalls. Summer was winding down its show with an immaculately slow sunrise.

"This is the room I used to care for my mom in," she said. I turned out of the crook of her arm to look up at her. "It was really scary in the end. I couldn't hear her over the machine she was hooked up to."

"Ash."

"No, it's fine."

"I'm sorry I wasn't around as much then . . ." I trailed off, letting my fingers graze her skin.

"You were in New York. You had your own thing."

"Still," I said.

"Still."

"I feel guilty."

"She loved me, and I loved her," Ash said. "There's nothing sad about that."

"Did you tell her about your plans for this place?"

"It kind of happened gradually. I met Indigo"—she looked at me before she continued—"and then I don't know. Something happened. We started taking in all these girls. I talked to them on message boards and followed them on social media. I earned a reputation for bringing girls here and setting them up with new lives."

"Recruiting them."

Ash laughed. "Sure, if you want. Or rescuing."

"Do you believe that?"

"Believe what?"

"That you're rescuing them?" I asked.

"A lot of them, yeah. We don't force them to come here. I didn't force you."

"No," I said. "But there was a pull."

"Don't trans women always have a pull toward other? Like, think about it, at a party who comes up to talk to you first? The straight cis women? No. The gay guys? Maybe. To call you brave or something. We have to take care of one another. Whatever the cost."

We stayed quiet for a while after that. I knew it was my turn to let her in, to talk about the things that bothered me. Lesbian trauma bonding, I remembered it well. When I told her about Ryan, Ash said that if he ever called me again she'd kill him. I told her fine, as long as we could hang his scrotum above our bed after and fashion a constellation from his veins. I told her about my girlboss encounters, Hazel and Nora's sad little love story, and Xiomara's dating escapades. She told me she wished I'd had better sex over the past few years.

"I'm glad you had trans-women friends though," Ash said. "I just think it's safer. To have people who understand you. It's so fucked-up out there. I've seen too much to believe the outside world is better than here."

When I told her about Max, I realized I'd never heard her talk about trans guys before. She only ever talked about trans women in an estrogenized paradise where gender was abolished through choosing one over the other.

Finally I told her my joke about the list of guys who'd cum inside me.

"My rapist," I delivered.

Somehow I'd managed to tuck my whole body into Ash's elbow.

"Baby," she whispered.

~~"I didn't want to do it without a condom. And then he was begging me and it was just me and him but I thought we'd said we weren't going to. I just lay there. I didn't move at all when he fucked me. He didn't notice. When I left his apartment he wrote his number on my arm with a green Sharpie. He made a joke about some stupid movie he was going to watch after I left." I wheezed against the wall of Ash's body. My joke was going south. I couldn't remember the last time I'd cried. "I called an old friend and she told me it didn't sound like rape. And I didn't have anyone else to tell. I didn't want to tell you while you were grieving your mom and I certainly couldn't tell my mom. It was before I was really close with Hazel and Xiomara. I was so alone. I didn't even realize how alone I was then."~~

I was sobbing.

Sobbing sobbing sobbing

So much of transsexualism is the divulging of history. It is not a gift so much as a bomb we're all passing to one another.

You may think that once you pass it on you're safe, but it's a never-ending game. You never really get out and you never really win. The bomb could land in your lap at any time.

I do not have a Great Theory of Transition. That's already been covered in every Tender, Important T-girl Book. If I have a theory about how the world works—and I don't mean the kind every boy gives you after reading two philosophy books—it is that the world is both more and less mysterious than we make it. If God is real, then He is the same. Both a simple carpenter and unknowable. Sad trans women rejoice, God is like us, one among us. When Paul in his Epistles said God gave him every burden so he could relate to everyone, he must have considered the allure of homosexuality. He must have considered wearing a gown, a beautiful gown, the very expensive vintage Prada one in your online shopping cart. But God asked Paul to step back from the ledge and he did. Paul's thorn was that he always wanted to be a girl. Whenever he shit in the desert or prayed, he was always wondering if it was theologically sound that he wanted to become a woman in heaven as his reward for such dutiful service.

"Fucking men," I heard Ash say beside me. Sure. Fucking men. I was glad I didn't have to retell my main Trans-Girl Sob Story. That one took much longer. At least it was more rehearsed. She knew how much it meant that I came to the commune despite my past. "Our kids won't have to go through anything like that."

Her eyes were black and wide with excitement. I hadn't realized I was thinking about kids until she said it, like something clicking into place. I didn't say anything, just turned over in bed and let Ash spoon me.

In the late-afternoon stillness of Sunday, Ash tried to fill me in on more of Herculine's lore. The commune was named after Herculine Barbin, an intersex memoirist from the nineteenth century who was later made famous by, who else, Michel Foucault. Indigo had been there since the very beginning. She'd been raised on a farm by her widowed dad, never told Ash her sob story, and never complained. They met at a bar in Bloomington and had been nearly inseparable since.

"You never mentioned her."

"I did, you just weren't listening," Ash said.

They were romantically linked for a little over a year until more girls came. I got the sense Ash had a wandering eye and Indigo was a little reluctant to give up what she had.

"It's not that I'm antimonogamy," she went on. "I just didn't want that. Or at least not with her."

Since then Ash had fucked most of the girls in the camp. I nodded, trying not to get emotional. Whenever Ryan told me about his past girlfriends I always wanted to cry. I used to cry in public all the time. Tears practically spilled out of me during my years in conversion therapy. After high school though, I only cried after someone dumped me. Ash didn't talk that way about her exes. She was quick to move on, like an acrobat, skilled at moving through extremes.

Ash continued recounting the inane history of the saddest homosexuals alive. But she'd created something. The commune was her greatest act.

I hadn't written anything worthwhile in years. All my work had given me in return was the nagging fear of dying alone. When I needed to Do Something, I wrote TV pilots. Still, conversion therapy was a hard sell. It was juicy in exactly the wrong way. My autobiography wouldn't budge. I chiseled at it in unpublished avant-garde poems and short breezy think pieces, but no one wanted the sad-tranny story. The zeitgeist had moved on. People loved the normie trans girl now. She's just like us, she longs for fulfillment through Hello Kitty stickers and investment banking. Every month there was a new profile of a completely regular trans girl who worked a high-powered corporate job. Freelancing was not as glamorous. I looked at the Famous Trans-Girl Actress and wanted what she had—the ability to hide in plain sight.

Ryan said I should like being special. Trans girls were called dolls because we were meant to be on display. To be played with. He said that I existed only as a constellation of desire. Or, that's what he meant to say. He could never find the right words.

Only girls who hate themselves want to be famous. Girls who torture themselves. Girls who want love in the form of praise. Anyone famous tells you that. Still, for a long time I wanted it. I watched my friends garner praise and felt intense self-loathing. He didn't support me when I tried to write; somehow, that wasn't what a girl was supposed to do either. There are plenty of ways to suppress a trans-woman artist.

Tell her that work about identity is narcissistic.

Tell her that the work isn't identity focused enough.

Say she's taking the place of women artists by masquerading as a woman.

Suggest movies about dead or dying trans women for inspiration.

Comment on her body. Slyly at first. Then just accuse her of having an eating disorder. Say she is fat. Say she is skinny.

Isolate her. Then tell her she is alone, because she probably is.

Underpay her.

Gossip.

Make her only direct artistic lineage into martyrs. They all died young to enjoy cult status.

Encourage self-destructive tendencies. Say they're beautiful.

Watch TERFs bomb her and do nothing.

Make a documentary about her.

Each time I had a piece rejected, I added a rule to my list. Sometimes while scrolling the internet I found new material without really trying. Hazel and I talked about it a lot—she couldn't understand my lack of success, especially in light of her burgeoning career. I didn't know how to tell her she was more cunty, more fuckable, more normie. I was self-deprecating and bad at making internet jokes.

"But you are fuckable," Hazel said.

"Not like you. You're available. They can want you and know it's possible to have you."

"I'm not fucking every girl that comes around."

"No but they can imagine it. No girl is fantasizing about fucking me because they know the likelihood is next to zero."

"Delete your pictures with your ex then."

When Hazel ended up modeling for a small trans-inclusive lingerie brand I gave her a lot of shit. I stared at the hazy baby-doll-aesthetic photos. But if I had that kind of success I would never give it up. I would go wherever the high took me.

We visited her family in Pennsylvania once. They kept teasing her about when she would start her own family. They grilled veggie dogs and set out strawberries with whipped cream. Her dad was a college professor and her mom was a retired social worker who volunteered at Planned Parenthood. Her mom said she loved my dress. I blurted out that it was half off at Zara.

Ash was still talking about the romantic entanglements at the commune. Apparently, Mira and Martha used to be a couple. Then they weren't. That wasn't very helpful or exciting. Besides, I could still barely tell them apart. I guess it made sense why everyone was mad at Natalie for "being all over Martha" then. Martha was into Natalie but worried she would end up doing the teacher/student thing. Indigo hadn't taken a new lover since the breakup. She seemed to mostly hang out on her own. Most of the others operated as if in a hive, flocking to the Queen Bee. My girl, no less. I wasn't sure if Ash would call herself that, if she wanted a label. Maybe we were more evolved than that. Maybe such allegiance was weakness to her.

"Is it hard to teach the new girls?"

"No," Ash said, shifting her legs over mine in bed. "It's like when I had to teach you how to finger my pussy."

"No it's not. God."

I kissed her on the cheek.

"It's more like when I taught you about hormones. Don't forget you're younger too," Ash said. She had transitioned two years before me. "You have such straight-girl vibes."

I felt her hand grip my thigh and turn me over. The beginnings of fall blew through the window. I shivered and she smiled down at me; I was going to be spending the season on my back. I told Ash it would be hard not having hormones for an undisclosed amount of time and she said not to worry about supplies. In fact, she admitted that she got horny thinking about giving me my next shot.

I thought about those days waking up next to her in Oakland, smelling her new pussy, listening to the sparrows, grabbing her strawberry pastries from the coffee shop down the street. I could build really nice glass castles out of very little love and in Ash I knew I had found something. Midwestern transsexuals bond for life.

"We have a meeting every Sunday and we usually divvy the hormones out then," Ash said. "Some I buy, some we get through other means. Girls pool their prescriptions. There are a few doctors in Indiana that are still kinda okay, more or less."

After a few more hours of fucking, we left her room and went to the main hall.

"Come on, girlfriend," she said.

I smiled. She knew exactly what I needed to hear.

The main hall was lit by lanterns, making everyone look beautiful in the late August night. The girls filed in and sat down in the pews. The temperature was just starting to change, the greens outside growing darker.

"Are you ready?" Ash asked.

"I think so. What happens now? Do we all take turns airing grievances? Go over the details of milking cows?"

"Oh fuck, I hope Indigo did that today," she deadpanned.

Indigo was the last to enter. Ash stood up after a few moments of silence and assumed a position of authority. She'd dressed up for the occasion. She was wearing a short white dress with lacy detail on the bust. Everyone seemed to be aware of the uniform, each in their own version of Sunday Best. I shouldn't have worn my combat boots. Some snickered at me and whispered in one another's ears. I was the new girl. Fresh meat. Ash squeezed my hand and smiled.

"I'm excited today," she said. "My *girlfriend*"—she paused and looked at me—"has come all the way from New York to join us. To see what we've built."

I beamed. She started rolling off some basic announcements before having Martha divvy out the hormones. As the last girl took a fresh vial, the crowd went dead silent, and Ash finished her opening remarks.

"Today we are gathered for the anointing of Elle," Ash echoed through the hall. "To celebrate her first year on estrogen," she added quickly.

I tried to imagine what anointing meant. Maybe it was some kind of lesbian ritual. Group sex didn't seem out of the question. I felt untethered enough to give it a shot. Sex was always a fun self-destructive habit. But then again, it was still unclear what Ash wanted. Part of me had wanted to get back together. But another part of me wanted everything to be temporary.

Ash turned to me. "Can you go get us some water? It's just a little ritual. It's gonna be sweet."

I gave her an uneasy smile and walked over to the mess hall. It was empty. The cook was gone, leaving only batches of dough proofing for the morning. None of it looked like it would turn out edible. Another girl rushed in behind me. Her small tits were nearly hanging out of a white tank top.

"I'm Izzie," she said. "We met earlier? They forgot a few things."

"Like what? Potion ingredients?"

"No, silly." Izzie giggled. "Dessert. We're celebrating Elle's hormone anniversary."

We couldn't find any dessert after nearly fifteen minutes of looking through the cabinets. She wouldn't even tell me what exactly it was that we were searching for. Eventually we decided to just bring the pitcher of water. Everyone in the chapel went quiet at the sight of the two of us reentering the main hall.

Elle was lying on the floor, completely still. Her eyes empty, her limbs splayed out around her like a murder victim. Ash remained at the front of the room, her pupils wide like she'd just taken drugs. Maybe that's what all the secrecy was about, the shifting feet, the nervous looks—keeping their stash to themselves. I felt my mind go fuzzy and my mouth drop. It had to be part of their performance. But the shakiness in my legs suggested otherwise. Elle looked like a perfect little corpse dressed all in white, ready to be hoisted into a coffin. The other girls were poised, radiant, and attentive, staring at Ash, their high priestess, with rapt grace. It was too much like church, some of the girls even held their palms turned upward as if in prayer.

"Is everything . . . okay?" I asked.

"Yes," Ash said. "Everything is perfect."

She helped Elle up after she finally started to regain some color in her cheeks. Smoothing her dress down, she found a seat in the pews as if nothing had happened. I tried to look happy. Relieved. But I felt something turn over inside my heart, something almost like an alarm. I shoved the feeling aside and sat back down as another girl launched into a speech about the "birthday" girl. I looked back to catch another glimpse of her, to make sure she was alright. But Elle looked like she was sparkling. Her skin glistened in the candlelight.

"And that's why I love her," the girl finished. "We're a family."

Something green and goopy was smeared on the ground underneath her feet. Ash saw my eyes linger on the mess and smiled, mouthing, "Frosting." The One with the Pink Hair brought out a green cake with a big number one candle. I let out a big sigh and smiled back at her, telling myself it was a coincidence. This wasn't like what I'd seen at the club. It was normal.

LOVE HAS NO EVIL IN MIND

No one made a sound as I walked into the cafeteria and poured myself a cup of coffee. I grabbed a piece of toast and left. The panopticon was alive and well, gossiping away and stealing glances at my unruly hair. I didn't scan to see if Ash was among the girls. I'd been surrounded by too many people for too long, I needed some alone time in the woods with a novel.

I used to read all the time as a kid to try to escape the present. It was my own special dissociative treat. My grandma was the one who kept encouraging me to level up.

"No, no more kids' books," she said. "Try Harper Lee. And Salinger. And this version of *The Odyssey* shouldn't be too hard."

I missed her. She was someone who believed in portals. That time and space could be overcome. Her library was always a safe haven from everything else that was going on. Maybe Ash's trove of books could be too.

When I got outside and looked through the oaks, I felt a chill go down my spine, an echo of my demon encounters in

New York. Maybe they were still attracted to me, to the residue of guilt and loneliness dripping off my back. So far I hadn't had any nightmares or sleep paralysis episodes, but I couldn't be sure that they wouldn't return. Every night I fell asleep next to Ash, terrified that something evil would appear. But so far, nothing had. Sleeping next to her felt good though. Like I'd made the right choice. Still, as I heard crows caw in the distance, I decided maybe being surrounded by people wasn't such a bad thing after all.

The chapel loomed above me, daring me to return. After the bizarre anointing of Elle, I was nervous to go back inside, but that's where all the books were stored. Bracing myself, I entered. The chapel was cool and empty. The effigy gleamed in the morning shadows. I finished off my toast and started poking through the books. The shelves lined all four walls, though plenty were still empty. Ripe for new editions. Ash had amassed a treasure trove of mystical volumes. Some seemed elementary—contemporary queer books about tarot that promised renewal—while others were dusty with pagan promise. Ash had a soft spot for 1970s lesbian astrology. There were at least twenty that used sapphic Wiccan wordplay in their titles. They didn't interest me. A large onyx-colored tome stuck out from its row, almost like Ash wanted me to find it. I let my hair fall over my shoulders as I started turning its pages, quickly recognizing her handwriting in the margins.

The tome prattled on about demons and their power. I tried to focus on the words but most of it was in Latin. I was worried. I didn't want to join some faux-pagan Wiccan lesbian group. Why couldn't we just leave the spiritual world alone? I guess for the rest of the girls it felt empowering to reclaim their spirituality, but for me it was another stark reminder of the past I had come here to escape.

I turned around to see Indigo walking toward me.

"Doing some research?"

"It's hardly legible."

"You don't speak Latin?"

"No," I said.

"Too bad. Would've been helpful."

I pushed past her. She was just jealous, trying to freak me out. My insecurities were easy to pick up on. Ash and I were girlfriends now, whatever that meant, but we were surrounded by her exes and potential lovers. I knew that as soon as I saw Ash my fears would fade away. She would tell me what I needed to hear, and I would steep in a world of bliss. We were beginning something new together. We were learning to trust each other again. I decided some sleep would do me good and walked back toward Ash's cabin. A little early-morning nap. Ash had kept me up all night again. She kept telling me to get as much rest as I could before she found a job for me. Something that would make me feel needed.

"Maybe even something with words," Ash suggested.

"Like what, writing your manifesto?"

She laughed. "You already read ours. It's not very dogmatic."

"I could do a rewrite," I joked, earning a big smile in return.

After a few hours dozing in bed, I drowsily opened my eyes. I felt vaguely uneasy. Something was off. I blinked a few times to clear my vision. I wanted to feel refreshed but instead I was consumed by a suffocating, low-level dread. Something was moving in the cabin, I just couldn't find it. Then, I heard something squelch.

"Ash?" I asked.

Silence. I continued to scan my surroundings until I spotted it. A mass of eyeballs swarming over the mirror in the corner of the room. The little enraged orbs had followed me. Each pupil was trained on me, staring, waiting, red and restless. I felt my own itch. The devilish spheres flocked closer to one another, jumping and energized as they wormed their way toward me like wicked insects across the wooden floor. I tried to turn my back to the encroaching horde, but found I couldn't move. I sensed a body beside me and hoped Ash had joined me while I was sleeping, that she would shield me. But in her place was a straw doll. A husk. Kindling for a flame. Unfettered, the eyes made it to the bed. A viscous liquid sloshed underneath them, leaving gooey wet stains on Ash's sheets. Just as the eyes surrounded my frozen leg, I woke up screaming.

After wiping away my tears, I left the empty room behind and walked into the growing darkness. It was almost seven already. A few girls walked past me.

"Dinner's soon," one of them said. I nodded silently.

Near the bonfire in the middle of camp, Mira was smoking a cigarette.

"Can I bum one?" I asked. She handed one over without a word and lit it for me. "How's it going?"

"All the girls are mad at me for one reason or another," she said.

"Like what?"

She shrugged. "Fucking. Not fucking. Wi-Fi being down. I tell them it's not my fault. But Ash wants more porn online, more money. I'm just tired as shit."

"I'm sorry," I said.

"I don't need you to be sorry," she retorted. We smoked quietly for a few minutes as the fire crackled. "I thought this was going to go differently."

"How do you mean?"

"I don't know. Sometimes I like it here, sometimes I think it's a whole lot of drama packed into a small place. Ash makes it sound like this is our only hope of being safe. She talks a big game about the far right but I just want some peace and quiet."

"Totally," I said. "That makes sense."

"I miss my ex. She was cis. Lived in Cincinnati. I drove to see her every few weeks before we broke up. It fucked with my head. I was making DIY porn when Ash contacted me."

"She contacted you?"

"Yeah. Then I came here and . . . I didn't handle it well. They had to tranquilize me for the first few days. By the time I woke up . . . everything was just decided," Mira trailed off.

"Wait, they tranquilized you?"

"Well, they put, like, Klonopin or something in my food. To be fair I was having panic attacks daily. But still . . ."

"Fuck, I'm so sorry."

"Thanks," she said before flicking her cigarette and walking off. I watched her disappear back into her cabin.

By my second cigarette, I was stalling out. I kept trying to find a spot to sit on my own, but the girls were everywhere. Even when I ventured farther into the woods I stumbled on two girls eating each other out. I wanted more coffee but that would've required talking to someone. Besides, it was late. Not that I expected to sleep again. I didn't understand why they were force-feeding some traumatized girl Klonopin. Why I was having nightmares again. This wasn't supposed to happen. I left the city to get away from nocturnal harbingers of doom. Ash was everything I wanted, sure, but there was something happening. Maybe it wasn't so bad, but maybe I just didn't want to know.

I stood next to my car, pondering what to do next. I'd go for a drive. Think things over, pretend to go on a grocery run or say I had to go help my mom. But when I turned the ignition, the car didn't start. It just kept turning over. I looked out the window like I was breaking the fourth wall in a mockumentary sitcom. There was no way my car was broken. Sure, it was used, but Nora had checked it three times before I'd left, and everything had gone perfectly on the road. Even if I'd bumped into the curb once or twice, everything was fine. I let my head drop against the wheel. When I decided to get out, I was careful not to accidentally hit the horn, realizing suddenly that maybe it wouldn't be good for the others to know I'd even thought about leaving.

No one witnessed my failed exodus. That was good. If I couldn't actually get out, they wouldn't know I was thinking about leaving.

I got out of the car and glanced down at my phone. No bars. Desperately, I tried to click every icon, anything that could connect me with the outside world. The group chat had been radio silent for a day or two and none of my texts were sending. My mom hadn't reached out since our last call. Not as far as I knew anyway, I didn't seem to have cell service at all anymore. If I missed too many of her calls, she would be worried, but I wasn't sure if she would do anything about it. Maybe she would know to call Hazel. But even Hazel only vaguely knew where Herculine was. Indiana was big. Also, if she somehow found her way to me, she might end up stuck here too. I needed an airbag, someone I could trust completely. But there was no one. I was alone.

It was nice, at first, to be out in the woods. To live in the moment with a bunch of other girls who had been relegated to the margins. But it wouldn't be long before the infighting began, before the gossip targeted me like a spear. I could already tell Indigo didn't like me. Cursing again, I tried to kick a rock as hard as I could and fell down. This was awful. I'd thought Herculine would be my soft crash landing but now I had nothing. No money. No service. No car.

Panic surged through my body. I wanted to scream, to feel anger, to feel anything, but instead I tried to rationalize everything away. The long drive must've done the used car in. I was having nightmares because . . . I always had nightmares. Plenty of people took Klonopin for fun, myself included. Maybe that girl had agreed to take it but had been too fucked-up to remember. There were logical explanations if I looked for them. I wiped away a frantic tear and told myself I'd figure it out. There was always a plan to be made, a loophole to find. I'd ask Ash if any of the girls were good with cars. I'd ask about the Wi-Fi and tag along the next time the girls took a trip into town.

I flicked through my camera roll to calm myself down and I found a picture of me, Hazel, Xiomara, and Nora standing in front of a melting wax sculpture. It was taken at one of Hazel's lesser openings. She'd complained that it was beneath her to display her work anywhere outside of the Lower East Side. Xiomara was grinning a bit too coquettishly and Nora was struggling to smile at all. I missed my imperfect little sitcom group. I scrolled to the next photo, an infographic.

5 WAYS TO ABOLISH THE COP IN YOUR HEAD!

1. Consider the ways you scrutinize yourself and others on a daily basis. How does this tie into your sense of security? Are you looking to confirm something about your worldview?
2. Ask yourself what constitutes "your property." What are the boundaries? What triggers you?
3. Think carefully about the things you try to control. How much of the world can you really control? Do you believe in bodily autonomy? For whom?
4. Keep track of the words you use to describe people you pass on the street. Who do you think of as your neighbor? Who do you smile at?
5. Whom do you consider expendable? How is this part of carceral logic?

For a while I was trying to pitch a think piece about the connection between leftist guilt and Christianity. Both were primarily motivated by self-surveillance in groups. There were clear differences, of course, but it seemed like a lot of transformative-justice advocates could not find a way of birthing a new world without equating a penis with moral failure. Mostly, I had questions that I hadn't gotten very far in answering. Like, how do we actually build a world in which vengeance is no longer needed?

And, why do we treat our friends like shit if community is one of our core values? I can't quite parse the difference between God, my conscience, and the cop in my head. I was philosophizing, something that people who are flailing almost always do. It is much easier to create a theory.

I stared out across the camp and saw Natalie and Martha darting furtively into a cabin. Two dragonflies flew over the moss, intertwined, mating, alive.

FERAL

The rest of the week went by without incident. Ash could see that I was still a little distant and things were tense between us, but I gave good head so she didn't push.

Every other morning I tried to start my car in vain. Ash kept saying she'd fix it and I'd even seen a mechanic come through—the girls watched him like a hawk as he walked around the camp—but I hadn't had the chance to talk to him and it didn't seem like they'd called him for me. I spent a lot of time dissociating instead of taking real action or talking about things. Ash kept asking me if I wanted to "decompress." I ignored her pleas, but I was still letting her spoon me at night and testing out nicknames for her. Nothing I came up with was as good as honeysuckle. Big Moon, Big Bear, Big Tit. She didn't like any of them. We lay under her canopy, and I listened to her complain about how unfair economics were toward trans girls. It is infuriating how quickly we adapt.

One morning in the cafeteria, Natalie asked Ash if they could talk in private.

"Of course," she said, motioning for me to follow.

"Something's wrong," Natalie said.

"What?" Ash asked as we sat down on a log a few hundred feet into the woods. Autumnal dew glittered on the moss, drenching the worms and ants who lived inside.

"I don't know how but my dad texted me," she started.

"What did he say?"

"He told me I was going to hell. I didn't read the whole thing. It was mostly gibberish, he was clearly drunk. He's a freaking psychopath." I must have looked incredulous because Natalie caught my eye and added, "No really. He almost killed my mom. She barely got out."

"And left you behind," Ash said.

"She left you behind?" I asked.

"Does she have to be here?" Natalie said, looking at Ash with big round puppy eyes. She looked so small in her soup-stained white tee and too-big checkered apron.

"Just let her be," Ash said, putting her hand on my knee.

"He nearly killed me too, before Ash found me," Natalie sighed. "I was on an LGBT message board or whatever and I vented a lot. Some of the other girls were too. One day my dad nearly bashed my skull in. That's when I messaged Ash. She told me to fight back."

"And that worked?"

"Are you so surprised?" Natalie asked. "Haven't you seen what we can do? The next time my dad tried to hurt me I knocked him into a wall. He was unconscious when I left for good. Ash picked me up and told me to learn how to cook."

"Which," Ash interrupted, "we're working on."

"What are we going to do?" Natalie redirected.

"First we'll get you a new number. Does he know where you are?"

"No, I don't think so."

"Even if he did, we won't let him close. You're safe, Natalie."

"I don't feel like it," she said.

"I know," Ash said. She got up and held Natalie in her arms.

"Can she go now?" Natalie asked.

"Of course," Ash said, dismissing me with a nod.

I wasn't sure why she'd asked for me to stay in the first place. I got up and walked back to camp, trying to comprehend what I'd heard. I wanted to ask her more questions, like, how many of the girls had she freed from abusive situations? Were any of these girls people who had other places to go? I wasn't sure why she wanted me to hear about Natalie's home life anyway. Behind me, Natalie looked like a little mouse in Ash's arms, crying out in vain.

"It hurts," she said quietly through the sobs.

"I know, I know," Ash said.

I stumbled away from their private moment and tried to find a random chore to take my mind off things. It was odd to see Ash like that, holding someone she didn't want to have sex with.

On Friday, Ash asked if I wanted to help her with something. My mom taught me that love was something you had to earn. I never understood why we were Protestants when it was so clear that she wanted to do good works so we could get into heaven like Catholics. But then again, the Protestant Work Ethic made denominational differences muddy.

"It's one of our side gigs," she said. "We're going to shoot a scene and sell it online."

"What?"

"Porn, babe. We're making porn. We sell it on a website, a little trans-girl cult-fetish thing." Ash clearly didn't see the irony. "I have to go into town and take care of some things, but Mira specifically asked for your help. Is that okay?"

"Of course."

My job was to stand to the side and record the scene Indigo and Elle were about to perform. I was given a brief sketch: Indigo and Elle were girlfriends, but Elle had fucked a man, so she had to be punished. Mira was going to help me learn how to set up and roll sound. We packed into her room and stared at the clutter. She hadn't gotten rid of her needles and Red Bull cans crowded against rolled-up anime posters and a few jars containing dead insects. She'd draped plum-colored velvet curtains over the windows, plunging us into a feudal frenzy for proper lighting. It took about forty minutes to gather enough lamps from the other girls. Mira had the exacting eye, I was just her PA. We spent another thirty minutes clearing the mess and arranging a few wildflowers in a vase. Mira moved a hentai poster behind her bed.

"So just to check," Indigo said, "you're fine with being hit?"

"Yeah I'm down," Elle said as she brushed her hair.

She was wearing a tight pink T-shirt and sweats. Indigo was wearing her usual uniform—a white muscle tee and jeans. The belt was a prop, carefully selected by Mira to give off a certain vibe. It dawned on me I hadn't watched porn since before I transitioned and now I was helping make it. Ryan was always trying to get me to watch with him, but I'd turn away from the screen, trying not to think about the fact he was watching someone else while inside me.

"I don't want my name on the credits," I said.

Elle purred as Indigo caressed her arm.

"I'm almost done setting up," Mira said. "Elle, did you put on the bra I got you?"

Laughing, Elle pulled down her shirt to reveal a lacy white bra with feathery detail. Mira tugged on the strap and gave Elle a spank.

"Alright, time to get in frame," Mira called. Indigo and Elle shuffled toward the bed. They paused at the nightstand so Indigo could rail a line of ketamine. Mira swiveled toward me with a blank face. She seemed like the kind of trans girl who was always angry.

"Is the camera ready?"

"Are you gonna set the mood at all?" I asked.

"What, with candles?" Mira jested. "Just turn the camera on, okay?"

I nodded. Elle looked at me like a delicious cherub. I had to admit she was a better bottom than me. She oozed the ability to take it. Indigo slammed another line.

"I think you should join us," Elle said.

"She can't. She has to shoot the thing so I can direct," Mira's voice snapped like a twig. "She hasn't even done her makeup. What would I dress her in?"

"Tall girls don't need anything special," Elle countered. "I just want to see her."

I was too flushed to say anything in response.

"Come on, Mira. Let's get the virginal little fawn in on it. I don't think Ash is giving it to her hard enough," Indigo teased.

She fingered the harness by the bed. It was for a second scene, after she was done spanking Elle using her dommy-mommy voice. I'd read the script and found it a bit too campy. Mom stuff can be hot, though most of my exes never went in for that type of smut.

"I don't want to hear it, she's off-limits. We'd have to clear it by Ash anyway." Her voice lilted as she said Ash's name, as if, like a witch, she would know when her name was called. "Now, get into position, ladies. We have a show to make."

Indigo flashed me a thistly look as she stood tall next to her cat in training. I looked back into the DSLR and made a list of awful things. IBS, dog funerals, my boss forgetting to send me my paycheck, Ryan's sexts. Anything to keep the heat down low.

By the time the first scene was over the room was spinning and I could barely make out where my toes met the floor. Everything was melting like I'd just done a bump even though I was the only sober person in the room. The girls felt closer than they were, as if our bodies were merging into one amorphous orgy. My hand seemed a few inches away from Indigo's muscular curves but I knew I was still standing behind the camera, fully dressed and filled with shame.

The second shot was supposed to start with a close-up on Indigo's breasts as she took off her shirt. Clearly she'd had them done somewhere.

"Get in close," Mira chided me.

I tried to obey but felt myself getting wet. By the time Indigo slowly entered Elle, I was too horny to speak in full sentences. She was telling me something with her body. I realized why Ash had given her up—she was just as powerful all on her own. When I finally managed to properly adjust the camera, Mira called cut. Everything decelerated around me like we were moving through Jell-O. I took a deep breath and scanned my veins like the roots of an old oak tree, setting the camera down on the bedside table. It made a noise like an earthquake. Indigo smirked. Like somehow she knew she had me.

"What did you do to me? Did you dose me?"

"I didn't do anything." She laughed. "Did one of the other girls give you a magic brownie?"

"No," I grunted.

"Okay. Well, you're probably just mesmerized by my beauty."

Every interaction I had with these girls made me think about the late-night *X-Files* reruns I'd watched in my mother's basement. Even then, while the smell of sex and powder still lingered in the air, I felt like they were holding something back from me. Mira and Elle cozied up next to each other. Their hands grazed each other's skin, smooth and aching. They were clearly not influenced by Andrea Dworkin's take on pornography. That much was obvious, I thought as Mira leered at Elle's lacy pink satin panties. SWERFs and TERFs alike would've had a field day analyzing a trans commune that made porn for profit.

Indigo wanted to celebrate after we finished the scene. I figured she meant something simple like beer, tequila shots, and maybe sloppy seconds.

"Let's do a sacrifice," Mira said.

"God, yes," Elle cheered.

"I don't think our newest guest has ever performed one," Indigo said, stepping out of the bathroom.

"I'm actually gonna head back to Ash's," I sputtered.

Elle grabbed my arm and smiled. "It'll be fine."

As we stepped over a split step and onto the grass, I saw the cow and pig lying down next to each other. The cow's head lightly grazed the piglet's as they snored together in the mound of tall grass. Mira stood behind us silently.

"Wait. Don't you need the milk?" I asked.

In my head, a supercut of cute animal videos played for me as I stood in front of the pearly gates. I didn't want to see what would happen next.

"The pig," Indigo said.

"The pig," I repeated.

Elle was already jumping over the red wooden fence. Indigo wasn't far behind, slipping between the bars and grabbing the piglet before he had a chance to wriggle away.

"Applesauce, be good," Elle cooed as Indigo tied a small rope around the piglet's little neck.

I watched with timid horror as the girls leaped back over the fence with him in tow. Indigo cheered loudly, steadily gaining momentum as she made her way to the main hall. The whole coven came out to see what the rumpus was about. There was no sign of Ash, who I realized would probably have done nothing. Maybe she would've led the parade. I had hoped they were pranking me but grew less confident as we marched on. My stomach soured and I realized the smell of bacon was forever going to turn my digestive track into knots. Elle slipped her pink fingers into mine and smiled sunnily, pulling me closer into the fray.

Indigo created a small hearth using rocks and twigs. Previously, the pit looked like the remnants of a campfire, but now it more closely resembled a glowing town square. Mira and Elle arranged some larger sticks around it and Martha and a few of the other girls finished by adding an arrangement of larger logs. Finally, Indigo took out a lighter and let the blaze erupt. I could've sworn someone poured gasoline over the whole thing. In a matter of seconds what had been a small collection of dried leaves and wood turned into a crackling pig pyre.

I watched the young cook Natalie take out a bag of marshmallows. Elle and a few others wandered over for their snack. Even though it was only six thirty, a heavy smog descended over our little estrogen village. Orange spires licked at the wood until they grew into a nice mountain of warmth. Indigo worked her way to the front of the crowd and held up Applesauce. He oinked and squirmed in her grip.

"Can you all see the piglet?" Indigo said to a flare of laughter. "Good. Then it's time."

All at once, the girls silenced themselves. I averted my eyes and tried to walk away but Elle grabbed my elbow from behind. She whispered something unintelligible in my ear. I figured it was better to play along than to attract any more attention. Mira helped Indigo tie Applesauce to the spit.

"Today we call on Hecate. We ask for a bountiful harvest from the Queen of Pride. We ask for pleasure and power," Indigo declared.

"Is she joking?" I asked.

Elle stared at me blankly. "Hecate is the goddess of hunting and animals and sorcery."

"I got that," I said.

Demon 101 was not a subject I needed a refresher course in, especially not from a brand-new trans girl with a golden retriever temperament. The piglet's squealing intensified as he hovered close to the heat.

"We call on you to deliver us into the new season with a spirit of plenty," Indigo said.

Her voice quivered in the growing haze around us. Darkness was closing in. Elle gripped my arm, sensing how badly I was shaking. Indigo turned to the flame. Applesauce squealed in pain. The girls cheered in dulcet octaves. The oceanic feeling was murderous that night.

Whooping erupted behind me as I ran away from the scene,

crashing into the moonlit woods to hide. I stepped over half-dug-up mushrooms and a tiny yellow egg lying on a tuft of moss, then tripped and tumbled over a thornbush. Gushing red blood dripped from my leg. It was already irritated from shaving. There was never any time to recover. Every few days some fresh hell awaited me. The girls continued to twist the knife of disbelief. All I wanted was one good normal day where everything with Ash felt perfect enough to justify staying.

An animal sacrifice was too far. If I had any faith in my car starting, I would've left straightaway. I thought about making a break for it on foot but I knew that the woods extended for miles and miles. In the distance I heard the roar of my comrades. Witches, every last one of them.

I braved another glance at the top of the ridge and, surprisingly, spotted Elle. She started the slow task of making her way to me. Between us, birch trees twisted around one another, their vermillion and bloodred leaves knitted together overhead. She sat down beside me and said nothing. I stared at her, matching her silence. Most of the girls ignored me. Mira was one of the only ones who even deigned to talk to me. Most of them seemed afraid of me, like if they got too close Ash might get upset. Something stirred in the bushes a few feet away and I jerked. Elle took my hand in hers and smiled. I sheepishly looked back down at the ground. I kept doing that, I realized. I'd become afraid to look the others in the eye.

"Are you okay?" Elle asked quietly.

"I was in conversion therapy for three years," I said. Elle asked me what it was like. I asked myself what it was like. "Can I skip this part?"

The slight tang of chipped Americana, wide sidewalks, hot dogs and coleslaw on paper plates, sheet cake sky. Lying down on a baseball field to stare at the stars, wanting so badly to kiss someone, to not feel alone. I struggled to tell her the details of my trans-girl sob story.

"Don't worry," I said, parroting my conversion therapist. "God is so merciful."

Elle was lost.

"Start over," she said.

I started again.

My mom walked in on me masturbating to a video of two bleached blond twinks fucking in a pastel-colored classroom. After-hours bonus special.

The conversion therapist she sent me to was named Bill. He had one earring in his left ear and dressed like a youth pastor. He always wore a band T-shirt. Usually a Christian screamo band, but once he wore the Offspring. I still can't listen to "The Kids Aren't Alright." We met on the top floor of his house, in his "office." It was a mess of cherrywood bookshelves, an old cherrywood desk, and tattered papers. At some point during our session I stared at the fireplace, caked in a surprising amount of soot and ash. Something was carved in Hebrew above the mantel.

"The goal isn't to change you, it's to bring you closer to God," he told me. He never explicitly said, "Love the sinner, hate the sin," but he came close a few times.

We discussed my past. Nothing too sinister at first. My lack of a father led me to homosexuality. I needed a moral center. My mother was overinvolved in my day-to-day life, she taught me too many feminine skills. My archive still has many blank spots. If I ever recover all of my memories will I learn the secret of heterosexuality? A dark family secret? No. I already know all of them. I rehearsed them into the narrative of my psychosexual development.

To quell my churning hormones, Bill suggested I see a doctor. He already had one in mind.

"Time for a Xanax, girlie," I said to break the tension. Elle was rapt. She wanted me to shut up with the jokes and get on with it.

I didn't grow up with the fear of medication that many do. Antidepressants didn't intimidate me, even if they should have. To me meds were the thing I swallowed to temper the oblivion of my existence. Side effects didn't concern me because nothing concerned me. If I was hungry all the time, so what? I drank more Coke and ate Cosmic Brownies. When I developed insomnia or slept too much, I just started waking up ten minutes before I had to leave the house and burying myself in oversize baggy clothes.

After I started seeing Bill, the straight guy at school I had a crush on stopped talking to me. There wasn't anything left to say. He was a high school senior with an actual life. We just had a few classes together. I was suicidal and obsessive, he had a girlfriend. He stopped suggesting books for me to read and I started weeping openly in the library. I met up with a guy after school who sold me pot and pretended to be my friend. We watched sexy movies together but he was a heterosexual wimp. I felt numb. I went from school to church to youth group to my sick sad walks. The conversion therapist approved of this lifestyle, though I never did tell him about the pot. I saved something for myself.

I crashed my mom's car. By accident, I think. I can't really remember. The fireman asked me what I was doing. I don't remember which Fiona Apple song was playing but I knew all the words.

A few months into therapy, after the psychobabble about fathers had died down, my mother stopped to pet a stray cat before dropping me off at Bill's. I always remembered that. A little, gray, mangy cat.

My mother told me I held coffee cups wrong. "I wish I'd had at least one daughter."

"Me too."

The waiter refilled my coffee and I tried to hold the cup like a man.

Toward the end of the first year, Bill told me he wanted to try something.

"Okay," I said.

He moved toward me with the sleek speed of a viper. I wanted to watch his blood being lapped up by stray cats.

He started to jerk me off. He didn't take off a single article of clothing. I watched myself cry from across the room.

"Weakness is solved by repetition," he said. "One day you'll stop me."

We switched locations, started meeting in a church basement. Bill was a peer mentor for a purity group. Men gathered together and discussed their failures, sometimes describing porn videos with trembling detail. Their grins tore holes in the wall. Their laughs ejected spit and thorns. I tried to put my guard up.

My mother started taking me to the church Bill ministered at. The hall was filled with votives. The sermons were long. The pastors frequently parsed out Hebraic spells, explicating the mystics and their wickedness. I didn't understand why the pastors talked about witchcraft with such reverence. They never had us sing Psalms. They mentioned demons with whispered glee. God was a minor character in their lexicon. And yet He was the one we sang to. He was the one who was always watching. He was the shepherd and we were his flock.

Bill had me whip myself during a session. He stared at me, soaking everything in. His hands trembled above his crotch. By the time I rang my grandma's doorbell an hour later I was wet with shame.

My grandma didn't ask what happened, but she taught me a prayer. She made coffee and handed me one of her Amish romance novels.

"This one is set during Christmastime. I think you'll like it."

"Thank you, Grandma."

"Are you okay?"

"Of course. Just had a hard day."

"Let me teach you a prayer I know . . ." She bowed her head and took my hands in her hers. "Lord, lead me through the mystery."

When I was seventeen and a half, I hooked up with a guy in the woods. He was kind. He was patient as we walked around and talked about the worst books we'd ever read for school. I said *The Old Man and the Sea*. He said *The Grapes of Wrath*. Taste.

After we hooked up, I drove to church in tears. I told Bill at our next session.

"It's harder to go straight once you've had an experience," he chided me.

"Sit down," Bill said, "I have something else I want to try."

He pulled out a knife.

"An exorcism," he said. He was smiling. "You've been possessed."

"Oh," I said.

I watched the candles. Mood lighting. I saw men without faces moving in the walls. I tried to memorize the classifications of demons from the sermons at church but it was impossible. The things I saw were like tulpas, manifesting whatever childish fear I harbored. I blinked and they evaporated but the ceremony wasn't over. Bill cut my arm and let it bleed into a little coffee mug before setting it down in the middle of the floor. He was speaking backward in a mishmash of Latin and Hebrew, swiftly moving from one murderous poem to another.

"Good night," he said as he drank my blood from the coffee mug.

There are many ways hairpulling can be fun. None of them involve demons.

I don't remember hitting the floor, or what ghouls may have swarmed around me while I was out, but when I woke, Bill said the exorcism had failed. I bit my lip and turned toward the window, hoping our hour and a half was up. He asked me how I was feeling and I lied.

"Clean."

"Good," he said. "Very good."

After the pseudo-exorcism failed, the church closed ranks. I was invited to go on a hike in the San Juan Mountains with the youth group. Bill encouraged me to attend. We hiked up stiff whipped-cream peaks and told one another stories about opioid overdoses and shotgun weddings. The stories of our lives, the tales of Midwestern midwives and coming back to Jesus. We hiked for eight days. Every time we stopped, a new hiker told their origin story. I knew what was expected of me—a conversion narrative—but I decided to be honest anyway. I told them I didn't believe in hell. I said I didn't think being gay was a sin. I did not try to sell them on a fantasy about a sinful, dirty freak becoming a good Christian boy. One guy found this touching. As we lay down to sleep, another told me I was a sinner and going to hell. Cramped quarters. I was trying to convince myself of something. Mostly, they ignored me, then agreed that I would grow up to be a worship leader or a teacher.

I was trying to convince myself of something.

On the last night, we slept alone under the starless night. We were supposed to be praying but there were three demons staring at me, I was sure of it. They started pulling my hair with prickly fingers that cracked with each tug. I was ruining my chance at communion with the divine. I was inviting evil.

"When I came out in college, my mother messaged Bill. He told her I should prepare for hell. Pack your bags, kids, we're headed to Sheol," I said. Elle didn't laugh. "A year later I moved to New York."

She looked at me like a therapist looks at a wounded child. I blushed and looked away. I did not want her to see me like this.

"I'm sorry, babe. I'm so sorry."

"I don't want to cry," I said. "Can I skip the rest?"

I was choking on grief. I could not name everything, drowning in a sea of velvet waves. She helped me down onto a smooth rock and wrapped her hands around me. She mumbled something about demons that I didn't make out. Probably her disbelief, I decided. I wanted to make her promise not to tell anyone but there was nothing to promise. Everyone knew. I was not special in my grief. And strangely, I was not alone.

After a while Elle said she was going to head back. I told her I needed a little more time. She just smiled, walked away, and told me to check in with her soon. It took me a few hours alone after talking to Elle to self-soothe, reciting a Mary Oliver poem and thinking through escape plans, each with its own faults. I made my way down a hill and ended up in front of the dying fire. The piglet's carcass sat in the charred ashes. Poor Applesauce.

SATISFACTION

I woke up in a cold sweat, feeling a crimson presence pressing against the perimeter of camp. Dusk swam in inky circles, forcing me to wait until the shadows took shape. Ash snored next to me, unaware of my nightly ritual of waking up alone and listening to the silence until morning broke. If I was a bitch, I was a good one. Our dynamic still felt uneasy. I wanted to give in, but I struggled to feel wholly safe in her arms. She liked to hold me as we fell asleep. When we had sex, I no longer came. Ash pretended not to notice. Still, I didn't feel like I could push her away even if songs of ambivalence were keeping me alive.

Sunday morning was quiet. When Ash eventually woke up, we cracked the window and had coffee in bed. We both knew in a few weeks it would be too cold to leave the windows open; we would have to cuddle for warmth. I struggled to look her in the eyes.

"I missed this," she whispered, nibbling on my ear.

This is what Ash offered—the ability to undo years of trauma with a kiss. Hazel always needled me that love was not a cure-all, but the way Ash tasted on my lips was an amnestic agent. I didn't want her to be the woman who was more or less holding me captive. I wanted to believe that everything was just a coincidence. The autumn wind blowing in with a few final pranks. But the aura of the camp felt hostile. The landscape of my nightmares easily mapped onto the eerie woods. Birches boxed us in like a ruptured womb.

I felt a Freudian attachment to the sacrificial pig. How long would it before that was me on the spit? I wanted Ash and me to be on the same page. I wanted to reach in and find the part of her that loved me in a sweet way. Not as a possession or achievement. It was jarring to remember us singing pop songs together in her car. The way she had held back my hair during so many puke-filled nights. When I realized I was going to transition, actually do it, she was one of the first people I called. I cried wads of snot to her as she told me how excited she was for me.

"The next time we fuck maybe we'll both have pussies." She'd laughed. That was a long time ago. She'd made the switch but I'd fumbled my chances. My insurance was shit and I could never save up enough for a consult.

Under our blanket fort, Ash tried to soothe me. I was feeling panicked. It felt hard to pin things down when I actually brought them up to her.

"I promise you we'll get a mechanic to fix the car. We're just . . . a little low on money right now. Food's been costing more than it should. Inflation sucks."

I nodded, trying not to feel slighted at being reminded that I was now part of a whole. She had many children. She couldn't show favoritism.

"The animal thing was weird," she said, making it sound like I was just a little paranoid. "I'll talk to them."

It was the first time Ash had tried to actively distance herself from the charge of organized religion. She told me that she knew I was sensitive to that kind of thing.

"I won't tell them it came from you. I'll just nudge them a bit. Ya know?"

I nodded again, tamed and chagrined. I felt like I had no choice but to agree with everything she said. It wasn't just what she said, it was the sweet tone she used, like back when we shared PB&Js because we were so broke.

"And I know the nightmares have been bad. I remember how they were in college."

Did she? I couldn't remember telling her about them, but I must have. She told me that I would come into my own at Herculine, that I would find my purpose.

"It's good to have a break," she said. "You can find yourself. Not in, like, a corny way or whatever but in a real way. You have time to focus. You could write. Maybe be our little scribe in paradise. A newsletter or a short film or . . . I don't know. I'm not creative. Not like you."

I'd thought about treating my time at Herculine like a writing retreat when I'd first decided to come. I was always too scared to apply to a real one, afraid it would prove I was a failure. It was like Ash knew I needed to hear that I could still make something of my life.

I reached between my toes and found a weed squashed against them. The day before, Elle had painted my toenails pink.

"Trans women regain their agency here." She kept using the word *trans* like a rallying cry. Sometimes it seemed like we all used the word *girls* instead of *women* because we were afraid to grow up. Maybe I was projecting but it felt like we were worried of claiming the mantle of womanhood, like girlhood was the best we could shoot for. Easier, somehow. When I finally heard her say *women* I realized how uneasy it made me. How *girls* felt less terrifying. Like a transitional pacifier.

She took my face in her hand and turned my gaze toward her. Sunlight crossed her chest in gauzy knives. I stared at her breasts, lit up like half crescents. "I do what I have to do so I can get what I want—what we all want . . ."

"What do you want?"

"I wanted the one thing you and I grew up without."

Chickens squawked as the day sped into being. A girl's voice floated near the window.

"What's that?" I asked.

"Love."

Ash left after she'd finished toying with me. I was a wet mop puddle splashing in her sheets. She seemed to think that if I was satisfied sexually then I would be okay and was clearly frustrated that I wasn't enjoying myself. Joy was going to be my inheritance whether I wanted it or not.

I grabbed a black T-shirt and a pair of Ash's jeans that I found below her cheap IKEA lamp. A half second later, I felt a buzz in my pocket. Even though my phone no longer had service, I carried it on me like a talisman. Every day I checked it for missed calls or texts and occasionally tried to send a few of my own, but most of the time I got failure-to-send alerts. I tried to tell myself that was just what living in the woods was like. Another buzz. Someone was calling me. I hurried to a quiet corner, hoping not to lose the signal before I could answer. When I looked down, I saw that it was Ryan calling. I would've preferred to hear from Hazel, or anyone really, but was desperate to hear from someone on the outside.

"Hello," I said.

"You finally fucking answer—"

"Listen, Ryan, I know you're upset—"

"Shut up. Shut the fuck up. You think you have me pegged. I saw you walking with all those fucking trans girls acting like you were hot shit but you were the ugliest one. You still don't have tits and your tattoos look like shit. Stick and pokes. You should've gone to my friend and gotten a real tattoo. You should've been there for me. I've been having a really hard time and I'm not a misogynist. I'm a good guy. You're just in the same girl gang you always were and you'll never get over the fact that you're trans. Also it's really fucked-up to judge someone based on the kind of porn they watch."

He was out of breath and gathering steam at the same time.

"Ryan."

"I'm not even the one who called it tranny porn."

"You like rape porn, Ryan, not just fucking tranny porn." My voice was an ice pick. If I could have performed a lobotomy on him I would have.

"I should've dumped you sooner. Fuck you." I heard the millisecond of hesitation as he contemplated whether he should add what came next. "Cunt."

Bisexuality was not all it was cracked up to be.

Of course his call was the only one to come through. The only other notification I received before the connection dropped was a text from my mom asking if I would be free to visit her sometime soon since I was living so close. I tried to send a response but only got another failure-to-send notification. Hazel still hadn't responded to my last text. I typed out an innocuous message asking her to visit, then instantly regretted it and deleted the whole thing. I couldn't bring her into this mess. Xiomara or Nora either. Besides, I was fine. Everything was great between me and Ash.

Ryan wasn't always so mean, just thoughtless and possessive. Once, when I told him I was waiting for him at the airport with flowers, he responded that I "better not give them to anyone else lol." I'd laughed and laughed and laughed and laughed. We never saw each other in person again after our breakup, but sometimes he joked that we were meant to be. A lot of my exes sent me shit like that, Ash included. I was cosmically tied to a lot of love, just not the kind that set me free.

Lunch was some sort of a green mush served with slices of porous white bread. Apparently we were practicing austerity. Elle motioned me over to her table, where she was sitting next to a girl named Esther, one of the few non-white girls at Herculine. Her grandparents had immigrated from Taiwan and worked at the University of Chicago. They were both quite religious, apparently. I sat down and dragged my spoon through the slime. After my dismal phone call with Ryan, I craved the company of the girls around me. Cutting off cis people suddenly seemed entirely understandable. Maybe they were onto something I'd fundamentally misunderstood. Plus, some of them were even kind of sweet.

"Natalie really is an awful cook," Esther said.

"Give her a break," Elle said.

"I, for one, would love some protein," Esther said.

"Maybe Natalie will get that shipment of hot dogs in, and we can have a barbecue," Elle said.

"What even is this?" I asked sarcastically. "Another sacrificial lamb?"

My nervousness betrayed the core of my question. The girls looked at me vacantly. Maybe I was taking things too far. Eventually they offered me a perfunctory laugh before continuing to eat up their filthy gossip and undercooked slop.

"I think Martha was flirting with her again," Esther said. "Which is annoying. I thought maybe she'd finally hit on me."

"You need a new crush," Elle said.

"And you don't?"

Elle giggled like a schoolgirl and turned to me. "You okay?"

"I will be."

Before I could say anything else, Natalie came over and asked Esther how she was feeling. "Any nausea?"

"I'm okay," Esther said. I noticed that she looked green with seasickness. She seemed bloated too. "Do you have any mint tea?"

"I do," she said. "But no hot dogs. And Martha's not flirting with me."

Natalie wasn't as naive as I made her out to be.

"Fuck," Esther said after she left. "She's gonna give us so much shit now."

"Martha was absolutely flirting with her," Elle said soothingly.

"Well, she'll fuck anything with a pulse."

"Are any of you monogamous?" I asked.

They both went quiet.

"You and Ash, right?"

"Yeah," I said. "Me and Ash."

CONSTANT CRAVING

A lake of fire bubbled below me. Shadowy snakes slithered and slipped over boulders and thorns. A lone juniper tree grew out of a small rock in the middle of the blazing flames. A child sat under the fruitless tree. He looked familiar, had scars all along his arms. He was covering his ears, trying to block something out. That was when I heard the voice. One I had heard for years—a savage force beyond comprehension.

"He is coming. He is coming. You will not expect it and you will bow down like a dog, humbled by the fire," it whispered.

I opened my eyes to find Ash staring me straight in the face, flinching slightly as if preparing for me to scream. I was, I realized. Screaming.

"Are you okay?" she asked.

"Yes," I said. I'd sweat through the sheets.

"Nightmare?" she asked. I nodded. "You used to have a lot of nightmares, right? Have they been any better here?"

"Not really," I said, reaching for a glass of water on the nightstand.

"Let's go on a walk. Just the two of us."

Ash held my hand as we wound our way over pebbles and moss. Weeds choked out most of the bushes as we got closer to a ravine that looked over a field. She always knew just what I needed. To be held. To be spoken to and guided like a child. My grandma was like that. She was the one who told me that the child in your heart never really grows up.

"I wish we had more one-on-one time," Ash said.

"Me too."

"Work's just been so busy. I had to code an entire website from scratch for this fintech guy. He paid well though. I think I'm gonna get everyone a treat."

She kissed me on the forehead before she dropped my hand and started rambling about budget. I couldn't force myself to pay attention. Every time I blinked I saw slime and eyeballs and serpents. All the demons of my past. My nightmares were throwing me off. They felt more real than anything that happened during my waking life. They were supposed to be long gone—I was happy. I was. Earlier that day Ash had asked me if I wanted to get something special for our room. I said we should go antiquing for bric-a-brac and she teased me about my vocabulary. We were building a home.

"Stop," Ash suddenly commanded.

She yanked me by my hand and held me close to her. I stopped walking and stood in silence, surrounded by fiery leaves and barren trees. I heard a crunching sound and noticed a bulky thing moving toward us.

"Down!" Ash screamed.

A bullet whizzed past us. The whole forest went still.

"Who the fuck are you and why are you on my property?" a Kentuckian voice demanded.

Ash must have gotten cocky and led us too far away from Herculine grounds. My body was pumping more adrenaline than I knew what to do with, but Ash looked calm. I turned to face her as the man in camo gear continued walking toward us. His gun was trained on me.

"Ash?" I pleaded.

Ash slowly positioned her body between me and the Kentuckian. She had no gun of her own, I already knew that. Whatever pictures she'd sent me before I came to Herculine were just for show.

"Don't move, I'll shoot," the man bellowed.

Ash's face twitched. I searched her expression for any indication of her next move, taking note of the slight downturn of her mouth, her left eye losing focus. As I watched, her head swiveled impossibly around on her neck to complete a full rotation before pausing to meet my gaze. Somehow the grotesque motion hadn't caused her spinal cord to snap. In fact, the contortion didn't seem to hurt her at all. Instead she raised her eyebrows and grinned at me, as if she'd just performed a simple parlor trick.

"What the hell . . ."

Swiftly, her neck untwisted to face the man, who was too slowly beginning to realize that we weren't just two lost trannies in the woods. He would not be going anywhere anytime soon. Sticky tar shot out of Ash's mouth, her tongue extending like an eel. Her body was pulsing with pregnant venom. The man attempted to dodge the goo, but when he screamed, it landed in his mouth. He fell with a loud thud against a large gray rock and stopped making noise.

Ash turned back to me, revealing her cacophony of serpent tongues. Each strand of Medusa's hair that sprouted from her throat waved hello. Ash's eyes were buried deep in her face, unseeing soulless roly-polies. Instead, Ash appraised me using her tongues. I could feel them burrowing inside me. After a few minutes they retracted into the dark expanse of her mouth, and I saw her again. Life reanimating her cadaver.

I never even entertained the idea that I was experiencing a psychotic break. I was already too willing to believe in demons, had seen and felt them. They burrowed into my mind, ready to shake me awake with the tap of a claw. Whatever comfort I'd hoped to find here to cloak myself in was just another nightmare—and the woman I loved was a diabolical consort. I knew she'd have some sort of an explanation, but I only saw destruction ahead. Fire. Death. Water.

As Ash dragged the dead body through the woods, I wondered what the difference was between self-defense, manslaughter, and first-degree murder. I hadn't watched enough law shows.

"It's me," Ash said gently, as if reading my thoughts. "I need your help. We can't leave him here for the world to see. Maybe some unlucky woman ended up stuck with this shit face and is gonna come looking for him."

I banged my head against a tree in protest and Ash looked over at me with vacant, bloodshot eyes. Maybe she knew something I didn't. Maybe she had control. I had no control. Nowhere left to go.

"Coming?" she asked.

I had no choice but to follow though I had not been comforted. The air had not been cleared. We made it back to camp with the man tied to Ash's back. Esther and Elle were sitting together and mending clothes as if posing for a prairie-girl photo shoot. Izzie ran out of her cabin topless. The others weren't far behind.

"Take his gun," Ash instructed, letting his body fall to the earth. In that moment I realized no one had taught me how to shoot. I hadn't even seen any of the girls with guns, as if they were merely props for the coming apocalypse.

Bits of the tar-like substance still clung to his body. Esther grabbed the gun. She didn't look like she knew how to shoot.

Indigo, Mira, and a few other girls came over from the main hall. Natalie approached the scene still holding a spoon from the kitchen. She was the only one who looked disturbed by what she saw.

After Ash offered her a curt nod, Esther descended on the Kentuckian's body, tearing off chunks of his flesh with her teeth. Blood stained the ground. Veins unwound like spools. I tried to look away but heard the unmistakable crunch of teeth hitting bone. She motioned for Elle to join her and my sweet new friend squatted beside her and tucked into the murdered man's arms and legs like chicken wings. I wondered what Nancy Drew would do if she found herself face-to-face with a cannibalistic cult. I puked. Then I puked again. Natalie came over and offered me a mug of mint tea, as if having anticipated my reaction. As if she too was disgusted, but only just.

"Horrible, isn't it?" she remarked, partly to me, but mostly to herself. But she never turned away.

Ash finally noticed me heaving my guts out. Most of the girls had returned to their chores. Natalie had left to finish cooking dinner. Ash took her place, gently rubbing my back.

Esther tore at the man's mangled leg with her fingers. I turned away. I didn't want to be complicit. Ash looked at me with pity.

"You'll be okay. You just need to lie down for a bit. You'll get used to it."

"Used to it?" I repeated bitterly, letting soft white liquid eject from my throat onto the dirt.

"You okay?" she asked. I took my time responding, unsure which part she was asking about.

"It was just spit this time," I said.

"Good. Good. Alright, honeysuckle, let's get you some rest before dinner," Ash said, guiding me toward her place. When we reached the bed, she asked, "You want me to hold you?"

"Nauseous," I said. "I just need some time alone."

The best lie was the truth. Despite myself, I actually did want her to hold me. But I couldn't get the image of her spitting acid to stop playing on repeat. Her head twisting, the tongues forking. I felt slit open. I had invited evil into my dwelling—gone to it willingly like a fool.

"Alright, baby," Ash said.

I didn't rest, the smell of copper coated the back of my throat. The feral sounds outside didn't help. "When the worst happens, remember your lineage," my grandma used to say. I lay down and closed my eyes to block out the sounds of the celebrating commune, but I couldn't drift off. I was furious. At Ash, at myself. This was not going to end well.

JAEL AND JUDITH

Ash had already climbed into and gotten out of our bed before I woke. I got up and glanced at myself in the mirror sideways so as not to see my full reflection before turning instead to the pine trees outside the window, stark against the peony-colored dawn. I desperately wanted to believe I was missing something, that it was all a hoax and Ash was finally going to tell me something comforting. She had taken my safety from me. We used to call each other home base.

I finished getting ready and walked outside to smoke and reexamine my car. I had to make a game plan, but I wasn't so sure I could leave even if I wanted to. Demons seemed quite territorial. When I was twenty-two, I had once been stuck in my apartment for forty-eight hours with a small demon because it kept moving the oil I used to draw crosses just out of my reach. But that was long ago, I'd fallen out of practice. The only demons I'd seen in New York were half dreams that dissolved after I awoke—except, of course, for the apparition in the club bathroom. But this was different, Ash herself seemed possessed. I did feel somewhat relieved, I supposed, that at least someone else knew about the darkness I'd long endured on my own. Someone I loved. Maybe I could save her. Exorcise her pain. Though, she didn't really seem to be in pain. It was almost as if she'd discovered how to harness their power. That was a tempting thought.

I went to go get coffee from the mess hall. A few of the girls were preparing to go on a hike. Izzie, Mira, Martha, and the One with the Pink Hair walked closely together, smoking clove cigarettes. Rumor had it that the One with the Pink Hair and Izzie were an item. I still couldn't really imagine Mira and Martha hooking up, but Elle told me that all three were probably going to top Izzie.

"She's the new bottom in town," Elle said to another girl, walking past me to go get breakfast.

Somehow there wasn't a top shortage at Herculine even though everyone looked like a bottom to me. I poured a healthy amount in my mug and stirred in some sugar as we surveyed the girls in the cafeteria. Natalie was hard at work being a good little waitress. I wondered if she was mad that Martha was going after another girl right in front of her face. Ash was shoveling food into her mouth as fast as possible so she could get back to her cyber lair and work for the man. The other girls blended together. Unless they were hot, obviously.

I flipped through the pages of a promising volume I'd borrowed from her library, taking in its carefully cataloged artifacts, taxonomy of demon subclasses, and geography of hell. I read about locusts and vengeance. Seeing it all laid out like that felt dirty. I closed the book for a minute and sighed before deciding to localize my search. I used the index to try to find an image of the demon I saw in my nightmares. I found him easily enough, though the drawing didn't seem up-to-date. The picture made him look like an octopus. He must've watched a Slenderman documentary and been inspired to modernize his image. He was technically considered a lesser demon, but I wasn't sure that I would categorize him as such.

After fifteen minutes of looking through other minor demons and beasts, I found a page that described how major demons fed on human souls. Apparently that was their whole thing. Minor demons were like pests, nibbling off the crumbs of the damned, but major demons needed a soul to maintain their connection to the earthly plane. Insane.

I slammed the book closed and marched back to my car. The whole time, I prayed under my breath, the first time I'd actually tried to plead with the Almighty in a long while. I turned the key, furiously trying to get it to start. Nothing. The ignition didn't even make any noise. I unlocked my phone and tried to call Hazel a million times. Then my mom. Then Xiomara. Nothing. I threw my phone across the car and got out, opening the hood to try to see for myself what was wrong with it, but I didn't know anything about cars.

"Where are you going?"

I looked back and saw Ash standing next to me.

"I'm leaving," I said.

"Back to New York? Without any money?"

"I don't fucking know!" I yelled. I didn't know I had it in me to yell at her. For years I'd been so desperate to get her to like me, to want to be with me, but all of that felt so tertiary now. For a split second, I was furious. "Do you want to fill in the blanks? Tell me about how some demon wants my soul and you brought me here as a sort of sacrifice?"

"I brought you here because I love you. Because these

demons can give us anything we want. Vaginas, bigger tits, new faces, money, power . . ."

"So you brought *demons* here to make us cis?"

She said nothing, just held me in her icy glare. I almost slapped her but fixed my eyes on a squirrel running back and forth nearby. The ground was damp with the morning dew.

"This is going to be good for you. For us. The demons work with us not against us. They give us whatever we want!"

"This is so fucked-up."

"Babe! Don't you want control over your life? Don't you want power?"

"Power? Do you hear yourself?"

"You've always wanted surgery. Now you have a way to get it."

"This is so fucking naive. You're playing with something you don't know anything about."

"You're letting your religious trauma get in the way."

I went red.

"Stop talking."

"I'm providing for my girls. I brought you here so we could have a safe, perfect life."

"You think this place is safe?" I was yelling now. I couldn't remember the last time I'd screamed.

"I do. We made a pact with the demons. We give them what they want, and they keep us safe. You saw it yourself, with that guy in the woods."

"What exactly is it that they want?"

I waited for her to reply but she just looked down in contemplation. I didn't fill the space, I wanted her to sit with the silence.

"Please, just talk to the other girls. Talk to Elle. She likes you. Everyone wants to be here. It's not a prison. I want you to stay but I want you to want to stay."

"Then why didn't you tell me what I was getting into before I got here?"

"I knew you wouldn't believe me," she said.

"Yes. I would have," I spat and turned back toward the car.

"They won't let you go."

"And how will they stop me?"

"It's different for different girls," she said, almost nonchalant. "They find a way."

"Why me? Why us?"

"The demons are drawn to us because the trauma we've experienced severed our tethers to the earthly world. It makes us different. More receptive."

"More vulnerable, you mean," I interrupted.

"Maybe. But I don't feel as weak as I once did."

When my conversion therapist started incorporating demons into our sessions, I did not put up a fight. When I was a kid, I didn't try to attack or banish the ghouls that gathered in my grandma's closet and under my bed. I let them in. I was tempted to do so again. For FFS? Maybe. A vaginoplasty? Could be nice. But I couldn't imagine fully giving in to the very thing I had been brought up to abhor, supernatural beings that offered keys to the kingdom of eternal night.

Later, I would say this was why. This was why love turned to rage. Girls know where the knife goes, something sweet to butterfly the lungs. Ash knew how badly I wanted to kiss her in the morning and demanded love as tribute. Saccharine.

"Remember," she said, voice softening. Her eyes were black and fully dilated. "When I woke you up in college with a box of powdered sugar donuts?"

"Of course," I said.

"Don't you see what we have here?" she tried again.

"What do we have here?" I challenged.

"Trans-girl utopia, baby." She smiled. "At Herculine, we can all get what we want."

"And what is it that you want?" I asked, trying to keep my voice even.

"I want you, honeysuckle."

Her words caught me by the throat. I left my car behind to walk away with her, past a big fallen oak.

"You can have anything you want. A perfect body. A book deal. Revenge. Anything. You can keep other people safe." She trailed off, seemingly uncertain of how to continue. I wasn't sure if she was heartbroken or just trying to buy time. "When I moved to Oakland, I kept waiting to feel this big moment of trans community. But all I found was more of the same. Everyone was fractured and broken and gossiping. So many girls had dated one another, and everyone felt like lines had been crossed, promises had been broken. No one felt safe. And I think a big part of that wasn't just internal shit, I think a lot of it was the way we were all incentivized to, like, compete for our piece of the pie. And then our piece of the pie kept getting smaller. When I had surgery I had to call you because . . . I just didn't have that many people to call. There's something about Midwestern girls. Indiana girls on Indiana nights. We've seen some shit. We're not perfect. I know we have some of the same problems—romantic squabbles, cool-girl bullshit, but we know how to stick by one another."

I agreed with almost everything she said. And yet I still felt terrified. The same impulse that made me not trust anyone had led her to build something. Admittedly, on a mountain of lies, but she had built something.

"We need more intergenerational mothering. We can't repeat the same mistakes over and over," she continued.

"Ash," I said. She turned back toward me, doe-eyed.

"What, my sweet?"

"I hear you, but c'mon. We're talking about demons here, and murder. It isn't all as idyllic as you're making it out to be."

"I know there's an adjustment period at first. But once your demon reveals himself to you, I'm sure you'll feel better."

"I don't want anything to do with a demon," I said. Ash's face was pure acid. I looked down. "This is just . . . a lot."

"The demons don't take anything from us that we don't already from one another."

"What does that mean?"

"They feed on our trauma but so do we. Trans girls use their trauma as a survival tool. It's a dissociation tactic, an art practice, a bonding element. It's how we fall in love. Isn't that how we fell in love, at first? When you told me what they did to you?"

I looked up in horror.

"No."

I sat in a field of honeysuckle straining to remember everything I'd ever learned in therapy. All the years I'd spent convincing myself that I was a good, normal, lovable person felt like a waste. All that time telling myself that being trans wasn't monstrous, that being a faggot wasn't demonic, seemed meaningless. Still, I tried not to let the fact that demons were real reverse those hard-earned lessons. If demons were real, maybe angels were too. Maybe angels were perverted transsexuals.

The dew on the grass was colder than I expected on my palms. I did not want to acknowledge good and evil. My brain was rotting trying to think through loopholes and ways out of the end times. To think, all along, the Evangelicals were right to scream.

Stars had collected in the sky by the time I found my way back to Ash's house. I wasn't going to apologize, but I wasn't going to fight. Girls have to be very strategic when they end up in a demonic love game.

For so long I though the only way I was ever going to feel loved was to get FFS, find a partner, and write something that made me lovable. Apparently, demons could give me all of that. The performative utterance of publishing a book. My old church up in flames. I could prove my conversion therapist wrong. I would not be lonely. I would be great. Great people are never lonely.

Of course I wanted Ash. But even beyond Ash, there was so much I wanted to do. I started walking back, still not sure what to tell her.

I stepped onto Ash's front porch just as Indigo exited her front door. I didn't look her in the eyes, but I knew that she'd walked away smirking. Ash came to the door and smiled at me. I gave her my best try at reciprocating and slowly walked up the steps into her arms.

There are not a lot of women heroes in the Bible. Ruth, Esther, Naomi, Rachel, Hannah, Mary, and Sarah. Then there's Jael, who drove a tent peg through her enemy's head. And Judith, who beheaded Holofernes so that her people could storm the enemy's city.

Do demons have heads?

THE ALTAR

White fire simmered in the base of the altar. Ash stood above it chanting in Latin. I was hoping nothing would happen. That I'd already seen the worst of it. Ash was in the process of offering gratitude for the blessings given to the commune.

I didn't want to go to the service, but Ash had practically dragged me over. She said that it would be good for me to see how they worshipped.

"You'll learn something."

"About demons?" I'd retorted.

Still, with no one else inside it, our cabin felt creepy. It wasn't a place I wanted to stay all alone, especially now that I knew what infernal stakes were at play.

Once I entered the sanctuary, a heavy wind kept me in my seat. A presence. I shivered. By the time I was paying attention to Ash again she was talking about the joy of giving trans women total control over their bodies. I had no idea how many of the girls had taken the bait. There were a few I could maybe see having gotten FFS or breast augmentation, but the devil's detail was exquisite. Everyone looked exactly as cunty as they wanted. I wondered what exactly they had to do in order to earn their beauty.

On Ash's cue, Elle walked solemnly to the front of the room and dropped to her knees. I half expected her to go down on my ex-lover. Ash looked straight at me. She had a pained expression on her face, as if bracing for my reaction to what was going to come next. I turned around to look at the other girls. What was the high priestess about to unleash?

"Oh, Asmodeus, Great One, Lord of Lust, King of Hell, we thank you on this day for giving us what we have asked for since we were little girls."

Ash was shaking in front of the effigy now. I felt a feather brush up my spine. It was the same feeling I'd had when I saw the slime in the bathroom and the stranger in the woods. A feeling that took so many showers to relieve.

Elle started to scream. A fury of words poured through my bloodstream like satanic poetry, slender curses like *bitchcuntwhoresluttranny. Dirty girl. You will be ours. Hell is your inheritance.* No one else seemed to hear what I did. They all looked calm, dutiful as Ash continued her sermon.

Leave.

This voice was different, nothing like the sleep paralysis demons I had encountered before. It belonged to something much older, much stronger. My head was splitting. I looked around to see if someone would help me escape. All nineteen girls were completely still, a fallen choir was waiting for something. The lighting in the room made them look translucent and seasick.

"There's someone new here."

My body froze. The voice was speaking aloud now, not just inside my head. The air in the room felt thick like stale smog as the other girls turned toward me. I felt dirty. Like the grime of youthful sin I could never wash off after masturbating to gay porn. I heard something pacing back and forth but no presence was visible. Elle was still writhing in pain.

"Little wicked one."

Tongue-tied and denigrated, I merely nodded as called. Indigo snickered.

"So you've returned to your home soil?" the voice hissed.

Again, I had no choice but to nod.

"All damaged souls seek reunion."

A plume of smoke sputtered out of the effigy into the lantern light. I turned toward Ash. She seemed to be in a trance. Her eyes were empty and putrid green, like two corn husks.

"We devour the broken souls of fallen girls like you. I am Dagon, one of many. This girl is promised to me," the voice called. I glanced at Elle, supine on the floor like a cavalier offering. "Your soul, however, is spoken for by another."

My stomach turned like a washing machine.

Ash kept calling for Asmodeus. Something metallic and rigid was bending in the air above us. My senses were overtaken by the sluicing of translucent liquid, the muted sound of cracking limbs, and a sickly green glow. I felt squeamish, like something was crawling all over my body. Termites and nausea. The whispers were starting in my mind again, telling me I was destined to die alone. That I was unlovable. I was a whiny, needy bitch. I was never going to feel at home in my body. I would repent for being on all fours. I would punish myself.

"Dagon," Elle whispered, her eyes trained above.

Emerald liquid leaked from the ceiling and pooled around the altar. Ash whispered to an unseen entity beside her. Elle looked up, her dilator still buried deep inside.

"No Asmodeus today," Ash said. She smiled, a wicked blank grin that showed off all her glimmering teeth. High priestesses were not the kind of women you wanted to go to bed with. "But we were blessed nonetheless."

She motioned for me to come forward. Everything hurt. Every inch of my limbs was speckled with sweat. I surveyed the girls standing around me—peers, jury, guards, potential exes—before landing on Ash. I tried to find the girl who'd stomped around the Midwest with me in search of a peanut butter malt but her eyes betrayed nothing of that person.

"Watch," Ash instructed, her lips turning purple.

A ghostly wind snaked through the crowd, leaving dust in the air as it made its way toward Elle. Her body contorted, broke, slithered. Fingers took the shape of violence. Blood streaked smooth and wet from her blue veins. The disembodied voice was laughing now, somewhere vaguely above us, a vapor devil. I looked at Elle, a demure little baby doll on display like a vicious talisman. I dissociated. This wasn't real. Ash wouldn't do this to me. She loved me.

A large translucent insect scuttled across the ceiling, pausing directly above where Elle lay. Everything felt very slow for a moment. The creature unfurled a single tendril, barely visible in the moonlight, down to caress Elle's body. And then, the rest of its limbs extended impossibly in all directions, shooting through the air and echoing in a horrible chatter. Elle screamed as the thorny legs pierced her body, working their way into her vagina. I tried to catch my breath but felt my body buckling as I choked back vomit.

"Dagon has chosen a new vessel! Elle will experience the miracle of birth!"

Ash was cut off by an apocalyptic screech. Dagon was not done. Elle howled in pain. She did not get to see her new lover face-to-face as he fucked her since he wasn't even fully on our plane. The tendrils pulled out of Elle's limp form, twisting around violently as they retracted into the insect demon's body. In slow motion, I saw one whip toward Ash with solid force. Without thinking, I jumped in front of her. The room erupted in a rage and I stopped mid-lunge. Then as soon as it had started, it stopped. The green light faded. The air resumed a normal temperature. The girls moved freely. My vision cleared, no hellfire braised my mind.

"What the literal fuck," I said. No one heard me though. I felt white heat flood and then drain from my body. My head felt cloudy, an empty tundra intent on not processing what I'd just seen. I kept looking at Ash but she was busy dealing with the aftermath.

The girls ran toward Elle, spotless again. As if nothing had happened. She smiled at me, showing off the glint of her shiny pearly teeth like St. Peter's gate.

"No one warned her?" Elle squeaked.

"She wouldn't have believed," Ash said, flashing me an unintelligible look.

Elle moved her hand over her belly and nodded. She was beaming with pride.

"Believed what?" I asked.

Elle placed my hand on her stomach and slid it down toward her crotch. There was a strange white mark on her pelvis.

"I'm not going to—"

She shook her head. "I have a womb now."

I turned away, letting my face grow hard with rage. This was insane. My whole body itched.

"A womb? To birth what . . . the Antichrist? What the fuck are you even talking about?" I exclaimed. Elle didn't say anything. I faced Ash. "I can't believe you."

Write it on the blackboard: I am not going to unlearn my trauma by going on a spiritual quest.

I coughed while trying to get up. Indigo stood over me.

"Are you okay?" she asked.

I pushed past her only to find myself in Ash's arms.

"Fuck you, fuck both of you," I said, shaking her off me.

Indigo looked hurt. I couldn't understand why. This was what she wanted, for me to understand that I was just like all Ash's other playthings. A sister wife, another conquest. She stalked after Elle, now the proud mother of a monster, leaving Ash and me alone in the chapel.

Flickering in the back of my mind's eye was the image of a strange doorway etched in Latin. Demons really need to get a new language, they've been using the same passé one for millennia. We've moved past holy Roman emperors and the Pope being the safeguard of chastity. Now it is the president of the United States, the CEO of Amazon, and that new televangelist from the Dallas metro area. In the recesses of my sunken dream, I saw the face of an enormous entity. The rest of the ghoul's body was shrouded in smoke, hidden within the newly opened doorway.

"Who's there?" I asked.

You can't escape me, the voice hissed. *I can get in anytime I want. You are mine and I am Legion.*

I heard Ash ask me who I was talking to but didn't answer. I realized I was crying a few minutes later as I looked over at her. This might all be a game to her, and she may have thought that I was hers alone to play with, but a new terror had entered the field.

CAMBRIAN EXPLOSION

I wanted my grandma back. Her God seemed more gentle giant than lightning-bolt-wielding patriarch. Someone who could offer comfort in the valley of the shadow of death, who could deliver me from evil.

When I turned twelve I went to visit her. She was, among many things, an amateur Arthurian scholar. She'd read almost every medieval text that mentioned King Arthur, becoming an expert on the man, the myth, and the period, and somehow managed to find and buy a ghostly Midwestern imitation of an Arthurian fortress. The castle was nestled on a tree-lined lake in southern Ohio. The walls were gray, weathered, and deeply beaten by time. My mom said a few minor improvements were underway, but they didn't seem to have anything to do with the foundations of the castle, just the furniture inside the house. Fancy desks, tapestries, antique chairs, that sort of thing.

The trip to visit her was supposed to be a field trip. I was homeschooled for sixth and seventh grade and rarely left home for extended periods of time. My mom was not the kind of person who sent her child to overnight summer camps. We spent our time waiting for things to happen on the moors of the Midwest. We didn't know what we were waiting for, lightning maybe, but we were patient. I wanted some atmospheric event to disrupt our tidy garden. I was being forced to grow basil for "science class." Outwardly, I pretended I believed our plants would grow, but really, I wanted them to spontaneously combust. I half expected and half hoped to return home to find my basil plant ripped out of the ground and lying limply on my bed.

My mom knew about my interest in myths and legends from the way my eyes lit up when Revelation was mentioned during a sermon. It was one of my less fruity interests. She was hoping the one time she caught me with the neighbor kid would evaporate. She didn't know yet she would have to send me to conversion therapy. The angels and demons of Isaiah interested me more than the titillating texture of Song of Songs. The kids a few pews over would read the biblical love songs smirking. Gazelles and melons or something. I was the odd kid out, interested in mysteries and arcane magic. As a kid I thought the world was a riddle and the Bible was the key.

We drove up to the castle in the family minivan, weaving between giant oaks and sugar maples. I was invincible, strong, and chugging Monster. The liquid-green electricity stained my teeth. I'm not sure what I needed all that energy for.

"Why?" my mother mouthed to me over my headphones as I blasted Fugazi. I shrugged from the Coke-stained, fry-littered back seat. We had the family drama rehearsed into a neat chamber play.

I refused the Frappuccino my mother drank and picked at the burger I was handed. I'd already completed one round of vegetarianism and would soon try to make another last. I threw my second Monster can into the trunk of the car.

My mom dropped me off with little more than a flick of the wrist.

"Here he is," she said.

My grandma smiled. She wore a seafoam fleece and a bunch of jangly bracelets. She wasn't the kind of Christian woman my mom liked best, but she did go to church regularly and always made us say our prayers before meals and bed. She just also smoked like a sailor and read a lot of lesbian poetry.

"Are you ready to learn?"

I nodded, greedy for myths and poems.

I spent some time poking around the castle alone. The ghosts that lived within seemed unusually active. I heard sounds everywhere. There were quite a few wings to the castle. Or it seemed like it at the time. The house had a single tower and many split-level floors, creating a ghoulish dungeon-like arena for hide-and-seek. After the initial tour, I didn't wander around by myself except to go to the bathroom. I wondered how one person could live in such a big place alone. My mom's house was claustrophobic in comparison.

When I came back down the large stairs, my grandma greeted me warmly, explaining she was making a roast and chocolate pudding for dinner. I smiled with the warmth of a friendly appetite.

"Before dinner we're going to do a bit of studying."

The room was littered with manuscripts, books, globes, plants, and inkwells. There was an opaque stained-glass window behind her cluttered cherrywood desk. Many of the papers had strange symbols on them. For all I knew it could have been alchemy she was studying.

I gripped a third Monster can. I'd come prepared. One always needed to carry one's life in a bag. I suppose that's still true.

I listened to my grandma intently. She seemed to have one foot in every world. Literature, history, technology, science, and art were all within her purview. I was amazed anyone could know so much about anything, much less know so much about so many things. My family and I all had our own vices. We each chose a corner and resided there. My mom loved animals. Before he left, my dad instilled a healthy constellation of conspiracy theories in me. I jumped at shadows, dogs, spiders, snakes, pain, lawn mowers, loud noises, politics, love, ghost stories, fire, slugs, and owls.

My grandma asked me a few introductory questions. She wanted to know how much, or how little, I knew about European history.

"Monmouth," she began, "wrote of Arthur similar to the way we think of him now but originally . . ."

Her lecture went on for a few hours. We jumped from history to myth with an agility I didn't realize was possible, careful to stop every so often and see how much I was digesting. I think it was a way for her to revive a certain part of her brain. At one point she had been a formidable scholar. She swerved to instruct me on the joy of Wagner. Years later I tried and failed to convince Ryan to take me to a Wagnerian opera in New York.

My little dopey brain could hardly follow the lines my grandma drew, a network of interlaced and undefined shadows. It felt like I was being told the population of an imaginary city. The onslaught of names reminded me of the endless list of names in Exodus. My only text for navigating the world had been the Bible. It was a raft, a canoe, a little explosive device. I didn't mention God that night. Neither did my grandma. Up until that point I'd met few people who disagreed on even minor points of doctrine. I had never heard someone talk about God or chastity as history. They'd always been living entities and virtues, not just words laid out in a field. In my youth, words were clearly differentiated as true and false. God and chastity were a part of the holy, eternal now. But to my grandma they were as vaporous as King Arthur himself. Moldable to the whims of a good writer. What was beauty in the face of a proper noun? To name something was to experience the magic of holding it. If we could name it we could bring about truth and safety. In the end it was all security theater. I didn't feel like I had a name then. I cycled through nicknames. And the kids on the block did too. Faggot was their favorite. I spent plenty of Halloweens being hit with sticks and stones.

After we had dinner, we retired to a lavish basement. Its modern sensibility clashed with the high strangeness that shrouded the rest of the castle. My grandma made us tea and waltzed in with bowls of a deep, dark chocolate pudding. It was so rich and velvety I have never forgotten it. She rushed back to the kitchen to grab spoons. She was swaying to Stevie Nicks as she balanced her goblet of red wine alongside the utensils. My mom never drank. It was strange to see a woman inhabit her body, to move with some amount of heresy.

After the credits of our movie rolled, we began to walk the corridors to bed. From the small room off the corner of the tower, I could look out at the cloudy, starlit lake. The water rippled a sickly phthalo green that night. The bedroom door was heavy, protecting Guinevere's chastity. I had no cell phone and had already finished my book on the drive over. I pulled up the covers. I was thinking about sex. It was the only thing I had in common with other kids my age.

I snuck to the bathroom to take care of a sudden carnal urge.

A few minutes later, I snuck back to my bedroom. It was

the first time I'd ever jacked off. I'm sure Lancelot would have had a lot to say. It isn't just me, he'd say, who can't be chaste. Shut up, I'd say back. His ghost would smile before heading off, dripping blood behind him. As I pulled back the covers, I saw a figure. It looked a little like me. Maybe it was just my reflection in the mirror. There were too many mirrors, I thought, trying to pacify myself. My glasses reflected some God-given terror. No castle is complete without a spirit unsure of its own desires.

The next few days passed by in a repetition of names. I was quizzed but I did not have the gift of memorization. I was often scorned for my failure to memorize Bible verses. I always twisted the verses into weird turns of phrase. Once my mom had laughed at me on a field trip to the Creation Museum because I said: "For God so loved the world He gave his only forgotten son . . ." A slight mistake with lingering consequences. The attendant at the museum had smiled, but my mother had swiftly corrected me.

One night during my stay, we went for a drive in my grandma's DeLorean. It was a prized possession among her treasure trove in the middle of nowhere. The radio was softly playing some adult contemporary song I'd never heard before. She sang along, rolling the windows down to feel the cold thrill of the wind. I wondered if Guinevere was punished just for wanting to be free. Freedom always seemed to come at great cost to women, while men treated it like currency.

Attempting to usher in a cheery Sunday morning, I slurped the last of the Monster I'd brought. My cereal sat still and soggy in a bowl decorated with strange hieroglyphics. It was my final day at the castle. We were ending with Tennyson. My grandma did not like modern adaptations of Arthur. I wasn't so sure what I thought yet. Part of me was married to accuracy and part of me liked the chase of confusion. I struggled to pay attention. Youth was a knife, urgent and shrill and then suddenly dull. It wasn't that I didn't see the value in knowledge, but I was often lost in the shapes and people shifting around me. It was easier to hide that way. I was overcaffeinated and depressed.

Before we began, my grandma pulled up an article she'd been reading as I sat in my pajamas, squirming under a pillow. It was an article about evolution. She asked me for my opinion. I felt nailed. I was being called to account. I was armed with information from my homeschool co-op and my trip to the Creation Museum. I tried to find a diplomatic way to argue for creationism.

"I . . . don't think that's real . . ." I stuttered, letting the words hang.

"Why not?" she asked. There was no malice in her voice.

"Well I just don't think it makes sense."

"Why not?"

"Well, what about the Cambrian explosion? Explain that," I said like I was landing a finishing blow.

"A burst of life," my grandma said, shrugging. "Many things that people once thought were magic, like Moses parting the Red Sea, are perhaps just things that science can't yet explain."

She responded with conviction, casting a gentle hint of doubt that Moses had even been a real person. It snuck up on me. People lead different lives. My grandma was not the same kind of Christian that I was.

I sputtered, "I just don't believe that."

Her eyebrows went up and she held her arms out. "Okay." Her voice was soft, like she knew I was twisting inside and wanted to let me be free.

We started going through the Tennyson and the manuscript

she was working on. A book. I didn't realize people could just write books. But there she was, writing a book in front of me. I remember thinking then that maybe I would write one day. Praying already felt like a form of writing. I sat down and gave myself over to listening. It would be a long time before I would come to see things her way, understand that magic was an everyday occurrence. Explosions happen all the time with or without a Lady of the Lake. I was lucky I had one to teach me the art of prayer.

SISTER WIVES

It was time to follow the hypnosis of need I was always talking about. I wanted to know what the miracle of a trans womb was like for the sister wives.

Elle and Esther were sitting on the front steps of the hall, while two other girls excitedly poked and prodded them with fawning smiles. I sat down with my sickly lunch as the cattails swayed gently behind me in the current.

"Can I talk to you?" I asked.

"Of course," Elle said, letting the fretting girls shoo themselves away. "What's up?"

She was wearing a white camisole and red running shorts, her hair cascading in a ponytail behind her. As we forked watery macaroni and paper-rot green beans, I asked her about Satan's experimental womb. Ash was on the other side of the river watching us. She'd hardly let me out of her sight since everything went down.

"How does it work?" I stared at her belly, still perfectly flat, and sat next to her.

"What do you mean?"

"The demon. The womb. I don't understand."

"To be honest, I'm not sure any of us do. We all had to see it to believe."

"And you believe now?"

"I have a womb, don't I? Listen, before I met Ash, I wanted to die. But when my demon revealed himself to me, when I realized that we could live in a symbiotic relationship with them, I felt power. For the first time in my life." Elle saw I was shaking and put her hand on mine. "I can't say everything's all sunshine and joy, but I have the chance to be a mother now."

"A womb," I mused.

"A womb," Esther repeated beside Elle. She'd gone through the same ritual a few weeks earlier, though she wasn't showing yet in her white cotton gown embroidered with sunflowers.

"When your demon reveals himself to you that could be on your wish list too," Elle said.

"Do you have other things on yours?" I asked.

"Of course."

"And making these deals with a demon doesn't . . . scare you? You're not afraid of the cost?"

"I'd rather enjoy myself than sink into fear."

A branch snapped in the distance. We had leaned closer toward one another during our conversation and the noise forced us apart. Leaves fell around us in quiet angelic crunches, but none of the other girls were nearby. Perhaps they were off participating in another orgy ritual. I ground my teeth. Girls and demons in a parasitic loop.

"The demon I'm tethered to used to talk to me when I was young," Esther said. "My conversion therapist told me it was because I was wicked for wanting to sleep with men."

"I'm sorry."

"I think most of the girls went to one guy or another. Mine was this guy in Michigan. We drove, like, sixty miles every week for him to do bullshit hypnosis. He told my mom she was smothering me. One thing led to another and suddenly the demon I was told to avoid became the one courting me."

Indigo walked over to Ash and whispered something in her ear. I tried to focus on what Esther was saying.

"Basically, I learned how to talk to my demon," she said. "We get along now. He said the conversion therapist ripped something open in me that only magic could close. I guess I do feel whole now, sort of. Full of someone." She laughed at the ends of her sentences, it sounded both giddy and terrified. "I'm not sure how they're related exactly but the demon gave me the strength to leave. Then Ash showed up. My demon said to follow her."

"I've never had an experience like that with a demon," I said.

"I'm so sorry," Esther said and looked up to me like a wounded robin. She cupped my hand in hers. I turned away. Elle was toying with the hem of her shorts, seeming almost embarrassed by our intimacy. "I know some girls have less comfortable relationships with their tethers. But I've never felt scared or threatened. Most of us make a kind of alliance to get what we need. A lot of girls realized that the demons their conversion therapists or shitty parents warned them about were actually guiding them to something else. Though it is true they want things from us too. We feed them in a way. Not literally. Or, like, we kill sheep sometimes or whatever, but not that often."

I didn't mention the man in the woods. His face flashed before my eyes, and I felt guilty about his fate despite the danger he had posed. None of the girls seemed all that worried about him.

"I just don't get how you can feel so positive about something that owns you," I said.

"Things aren't that clear-cut. We're not owned necessarily, we're tethered. Once we pledge our allegiance to them we're in a partnership," Elle explained.

"Mmm," I intoned, trying to keep a straight face.

"You'd be a great mom," Elle told me. Something small twisted in my gut.

"But you feel normal? Like you're having a normal baby?"

"Of course it's a normal baby. My demon wanted me to experience the joy of motherhood. He did it himself. I'm a month along. Ash has been getting me prenatal vitamins."

"And that works?"

Elle took a deep breath and turned my chin to face her.

"I thought about being a mom my whole life," she said. "When I was six, my sister got a baby doll for her birthday. She wore a little mint green jumper and had two big buck teeth. I spent months trying to find a way to get one for myself until one day I just took it. I played with it in the woods all afternoon. The next day, when my sister asked me if I'd seen her doll, I didn't say anything. I just kept going back into the woods in secret to play with her. Later, when other boys were watching porn and sneaking around on Reddit, I was reading about womb transplants and erasing my browser history. Of course, they found out anyway. Then I got kicked out and . . . here I am."

Esther smiled. "Here we are. You could be like us. You could have a kid."

"Do you think you want kids?" Elle asked.

"I don't know," I answered, wondering where she might be going with this line of questioning. "My grandmother always told me I'd be a good parent."

"Does she know you're trans?"

"No. She died before I came out."

"Motherhood's so ancestral. I loved my mom. She loved me the best she could."

"What happened to her?"

"She had really aggressive cancer. I hope I can give back to my child what she gave to me. I want her to feel just as loved." She stopped.

"You know it's going to be a girl?"

"No." She smiled. "No, I guess I don't. What about your mom? What was she like?"

It was not a question I could answer succinctly. Mom was a signifier to me. The word brought up a whirlpool. Ash's words from years earlier clouded my heart. The way she was so certain about motherhood. I wanted someone to be that sure about me. The way everyone at Herculine talked about kids scared me. I worried about the ethics of bringing up a kid in a world with revenge porn and demons and climate change.

"Here," Esther said. "Feel."

Before I could decline, I saw Ash waving me over.

"I think I have to go," I said, avoiding the hurt look in Esther's eye.

The breeze was picking up anyway. Elle turned to go and find a blanket. Some of the girls had made plans to stargaze later that night but I declined. I wasn't done clearing my head. Rupture wasn't as enlightening as I'd expected.

Ash and Indigo were smiling as I sauntered up and asked what was going on.

"I know you two have some tension between you," Ash said. "And I think it's time you worked it out. Indigo wants to bury the hatchet and teach you some hunting skills. I think it's a good idea. You could be useful. Besides, I want her to see how special you are."

"I am useful," I said.

Both of them shot me a dirty look. Ash slapped my ass and laughed. "Just go. Get me something for dinner. I'm craving veal."

"Well," Indigo said, "let's get on with it."

Half an hour later, Indigo and I were walking through a dense thicket populated by birches and prickly shrubs, silently nursing our own grievances. The hill we descended led right up to a large farm a few miles away from the commune. Indigo seemed to think it was far enough away that no one would suspect anything. Cults always grew bolder right before their last big heist.

"So you're really buying into this whole cult thing, huh?" I asked.

"Shut up," Indigo hissed.

"What? You're not going to try to sell me on how you're all just one big happy family?"

"Family?" she repeated incredulously. She stopped moving and stared at the weeds by her boots. "My *family* told me they'd rather tell everyone I died than say I transitioned."

"Are you in touch?"

Indigo snorted. Something in her body language made me want to lunge at her. Branches scratched our shoulders as we stepped closer to each other to avoid the brambles.

"Whatever you're trying to get out of me, you won't. I'm not going to launch into my sob story like the other girls," she said, quietly enough that it was hard to hear her over our footsteps.

"Alright. Then start with how you got here."

"By the time Ash started Herculine we were already together. In a real way. We got up every morning, made the bed, and ate breakfast together. She never cooked, I always made her eggs and coffee. I was there when her mom died. I was there when she decided to start this." Indigo gestured back toward where we'd come from.

"How'd you meet exactly?"

"I followed her on Instagram after we both got a stick and poke from the same girl."

A few hundred feet away, something large scuttled in the brush. Indigo put her hand against my chest to stop me from moving forward. I watched as Indigo took slow steps toward the noise. I couldn't make out what had produced it. Blackbirds broke free from the birch in front of us and flew up toward the sunlight. Two foxes darted out to my right over the clover and into a thick bush. Green sludge dripped from the bark of a large nearby pine tree. I tried to motion to her, but she was looking in a different direction. Soon, I lost sight of her as she disappeared among the trees. Alone, the woods felt too quiet. Then, almost as soon as the tension had gathered, it dissipated. Her broad bare shoulders flashed between the thick foliage as she made her way back to me.

"It wasn't a deer," she said.

"What was it?"

She passed me, saying nothing.

"We should get back. The deer are already seeking shelter," Indigo said.

"Do you even know what you're talking about?"

Finally she smiled. "I know everything."

"Except how to keep your girlfriend happy," I retorted.

Her face strained. "So, have you entered into any deals with the devil?"

"I guess. But Hecate isn't like that. It isn't really her style. She's not as involved as the others."

"But you're tethered? Whatever that means."

"Yes. It just means a demon has laid claim to you, usually because something fucked-up happened when you were younger. They wait until you're ready to cut a deal."

"Did you have to give something up?"

She wouldn't look me in the eye anymore. I knew I didn't have long before the power balance tipped in her favor again.

"Of course," she said. "Just because I'm going along with it doesn't mean I'm perfectly comfortable with it. Anyway, I'm not your mentor. Why aren't you grilling Ash about this stuff?"

She had me there. I walked alongside her in silence, staring at her taut body. Violent rain broke. Icy crystal spires shredded the wood. We ran for cover, landing in a small limestone cave. Thankfully the hills housed a few outcroppings of white rocks, fungi, and moss. Millions of bugs scampered away from our boots as we stepped farther inside.

"How long ago were you tethered?" I asked as we watched the shower. The rain shrouded the vegetation.

"Probably a few weeks after we built all of this. That's when Asmodeus first visited Ash," Indigo said. "You're not going to get me to like you. I know that's what Ash wants."

"That's fine, I don't like you either." After a minute I added, "And I'm not jealous of you."

"Then why even mention it?" Her face crinkled and I couldn't help but smile too. "What's your story?"

"Conversion therapy. Absent dad. I know Ash from before," I said. "A long time ago."

"She romanticizes that a bit," Indigo said.

"I do too," I said.

"Well at least you know what caused your demon to latch on to you. Some girls get lost in that maze."

"I do that anyway. I don't need demons to torture me into it," I said.

"I never went to conversion therapy, thank god. I transitioned young, went to Planned Parenthood, got a job at a thrift shop," she said, glancing down at the bugs. Worms erupted from the mushy earth with glee. "But I did get a lot of shit from my first boyfriend."

The rain eased. Enough that we could run back and only be soaked instead of drenched. Squirrels had returned to their task of gathering goods on the wet forest floor. We prepared ourselves to make a break for it.

"Was he what tethered you?"

"No," she said. "I think it was Ash."

PUPPET MASTER

Would You Still Love Me If I Was a Worm?
Would You Still Love Me If I Was Possessed?
Would You Still Love Me If I Was (Briefly) a Cannibal?
Would You Still Love Me If I Hated You as Much as I Loved You?

Sometimes I awoke to the intrusive thought of headlines in the newspaper announcing that I was dead. I was just glad I had yet to summon the ten-horned beast of Daniel. It only seemed a matter of time before more apocalyptic beasts conquered our green pastures and still waters. The vision of Legion scratched my amygdala. Even if I made it out of Herculine, would I continue to be pursued by some demonic force beyond comprehension? Surely they weren't tied to human geography. I'd spent the last few days thinking over everything Indigo had said when we'd walked in the woods together, terrified of what was to come. I even tried to start my car again. Nothing. Even worse, my phone, though it had been almost entirely useless to me, had vanished.

When I woke up, the nightstand was empty save Ash's tiny green mid-century modern lamp. I looked below the bed and all through the cabin. Behind books, under rugs, all over the hand-built shelves. Nothing. Someone must have taken it. Maybe Ash. If she was capable of murder, it didn't seem that far of a leap. The grotesque image of her face spinning around was forever imprinted in my memory. I was going to confront her but then wondered what the point was. We were already on thin ice after I saw her kill a man in cold blood. And even if I had my phone, it was unclear if it would work.

Legion was starting to interfere with the flow of space and time. I could feel his presence, always waiting somewhere deep in my heart. I was like a lab rat, stuck in my cage.

A few days later, I decided to go on a sojourn to sort things out. The woods felt impenetrable, and I was afraid to scramble around the countryside by myself after my encounter with the wild hunter, but I was more afraid to be around the group. I felt like the girls could turn against me at any moment and tear my flesh off in little clumps to curb their cannibalistic hunger.

Pacing around the woods and smoking stolen cigarettes, I kept hoping I would find a viable escape plan buried deep in my brain. I had too many dangling questions, ones that demanded real answers and spiritual guidance. I just needed to understand something. Anything. How a decent girl could build an alliance with a demon, how my ex had turned into my girlfriend and then performed a human sacrifice, how I was still anywhere within a hundred miles of her.

Hazel wouldn't believe me if I told her what had happened here. No one would. Maybe she wouldn't come to my rescue even if she did believe me. I wouldn't want to go into the depths of a hell realm to rescue her. Though I think I would have. I had the advantage of experience though. With cults and ghosts and witches. I thought my previous encounters had made me more careful, but maybe they just made me vulnerable. Ready to fall for the same shit all over again. I clenched my fist harder.

I walked the last mile back to camp alone. Ash was sitting on a log talking to Izzie. Her hand was on her thigh, moving back and forth. I didn't think it made sense for Izzie to be wearing a white dress in this chill. Not unless she was a sacrifice, a virgin, or both. But Izzie didn't look like either. I watched Ash's hand press against the girl's shoulder with tender reassurance. There was nothing to save her from, not really. She was doing this of her own volition. To hurt me. After I stood pouting for a moment Ash came over.

"What's up?"

"Was just out on a walk," I said. "Who's that girl you were talking to?"

"Izzie. You met her already. She got here not long before you did and she had some questions."

"Oh."

Ash started whistling "Will You Still Love Me Tomorrow" as we walked the few yards to her cabin. Somehow girls like her always knew how to make doo-wop songs sound ominous. Indigo walked by us, brushing past me slightly on her way. I realized that she'd slipped me a piece of paper. I immediately locked myself in the bathroom. From the other side of the door, Ash told me all about how Izzie was such a nice friend and a good person to talk to, someone who really understood the mission of the commune. I turned on the sink faucet to hide my tears. They weren't that loud, but I didn't want to alarm her. I wasn't sure how much of the performance was for her or me. I unfolded the little note. It was an invitation to meet Indigo by the split stump right after dinner. Usually Ash was busy then, advising the girls as they took turns airing their dirty laundry. Indigo and I never participated, so we usually had the time free.

I walked out and squeezed Ash's tits before spitting in her mouth and dragging her back to our cabin. As I shut the door behind us, I tore off her pants and went down on her. Just like that, where she stood in front of the mirror. Her hands darted around my uncombed hair, pulling and tugging. I dug my tongue in deeper, immobilizing her. She was mine now. I wanted her silence. Just once. I couldn't top her, it wasn't in my repertoire, but I clawed a long scratch down her left leg, piercing her trans tattoos and the regrettable little anime bunny she'd gotten at sixteen.

"Wait," she gasped. "I want to go longer."

But I'd already gone, leaving her to call after me from the open windows. As she slumped against the ground, I saw two skunks walking side by side in the tall grass.

With my phone missing, there was no easy way to warn Indigo that I was running late. Not that we'd even had a chance to do the awkward number exchange. The split stump was a mile into the woods, and I was already running behind. I was also not an outdoorsy girl. The few weeks I'd been at Herculine had not yet persuaded me to become one, not even after Indigo's scathing remarks about my shortcomings.

I saw her black combat boots glinting in the moonlight first. Then, her ripped jeans and black Yeah Yeah Yeahs hoodie. She had clearly seen me coming from a mile away.

"You came," Indigo said incredulously.

"Of course."

"I thought you might be completely under her thumb. She made it seem like you were."

"Not yet," I said, letting the words puff out nebulously. "Is this the part where you tell me what you want?"

"Look, I don't like you. But I also know what you're going through . . . being her little pet."

"So, what, you brought me here to give me relationship advice?"

"What? No. I brought you here to tell you what no one else will. It's true that a demon has already laid claim to you, that it will soon reveal itself to you in all its glory. But the key is that until that happens, you're still a little free."

"Free?"

"I'm sure it doesn't feel like it, but you could leave," she said, looking at the ground. "Most of us are fully tethered now. Maybe all of us, besides Ash. I've lost count. We can't leave unless our demons let us. But it's not too late for you."

I struggled to understand how Ash could be untethered and had done the things I'd seen her do.

"I don't believe you," I said.

"She's counting on that—your loyalty, that you think you have no choice. She needs you to stay until you're fully tethered. That's what happened to me. When Ash and I broke up, it was like the last twig of my family tree snapped. I was alone. That's when Hecate found her way in. I think Ash knew about the demons for a long time before that, like, even before she created this place. I mean, don't get me wrong, I think she believes this *is* trans-girl utopia: getting what she wants, freedom from some shitty cis hell. But we don't all feel that way. Some of us want out."

I felt my spine convulse.

"So what's your big plan?" I asked finally.

"Use the demons like they use us, like Ash does. Fight our way out if we have to. I don't know what will happen when we leave, not really," Indigo said. "Our demons will probably come with us unless we find some way to untether from them. I'm used to it now though. It's nice to have power, someone to talk to. I just need to get out of here. I'm tired of watching her storm around like she owns us. I think . . . I think Asmodeus is giving her special powers."

"What do you mean?"

"She just . . . has a way about her. Not just with you. But with the other girls. It feels impossible not to be charmed by her, right? She always seems to know what you're thinking?"

"I . . . I don't know."

"Well, think about it. She's awfully perceptive for someone so obsessed with herself."

"I don't think she's that bad."

Indigo shifted her stance.

"Maybe not. But she's not the person she once was. She's been feeding on something. And something's been feeding on her too. It's doing things to her."

Indigo was standing right in front of me, our bodies only a few feet apart from each other. I fell down from the log I was standing on.

"Why are you telling me all this?"

Her eyes narrowed and she turned away for a moment, vicious and alert once again.

"If you sell us out, I'll kill you. But I don't think you will. I'm guessing you're not feeling so pumped on that T4T love energy right now," Indigo said as she flashed me a crooked smile, but her voice cracked with desperation. "I want out. You seem like you can make it happen. You're the least tethered to this cursed fucking place . . . and you're her favorite toy right now."

"Jealous?" I asked, stone-faced. I was trying to come to grips with my ex-girlfriend's fickle heart. There would always be a part of me that loved her. That wanted her to love me. We were two fish, struggling against each other's currents.

"A little," Indigo replied. I jerked up to meet her gaze. She smirked. "I bet she thinks you're easy to please."

"She probably does."

"What do you really want?"

"Ind—"

Indigo grabbed my legs from underneath me and flipped me over, so my ass was in clear view. I winced as she pulled down my pants and kissed my cheek. She spit on her fingers and had me suck them. I automatically took them in my mouth as my eyes glazed over in lust. I remembered watching her fuck for the cameras. How intoxicating it was even though I didn't want to like it. She dug her slick finger inside me until my body crumpled with a gasp.

"Do you want more?"

"Yes," I whispered.

"Good girl," she said, feeling her way inside me, getting acquainted with what made me buck. "I don't think she's properly stretched you out. I bet I can go farther than she's used to."

"Stop talking," I said.

"I'll do whatever I want."

Her free hand found its way under my shirt and started circling my nipple as her finger slid in and out of me faster than before. I let out a moan. I hadn't moaned since the first time Ash fucked me at Herculine. Originally I came to Herculine under the guise of an orgasm a day.

"You should leave your little nest more often," Indigo said. "I could have a lot of fun with you."

The wind shifted, causing both of us to pause. After a minute of stillness, Indigo seemed to reason that nothing was out there. I was less certain but her hand clamped down on my nipple harder and the finger inside me turned into two.

"You don't need lube, do you?"

I didn't respond.

"Do you?" she asked again.

"No!"

"Okay then." She tilted my head back toward her, straining my neck with a crackling ache. "If you need something from me you have to say. Got it?"

"Yes."

"Yes, *sir*."

"Yes, sir," I repeated. It didn't seem like the time to question her gender politic. Indigo twisted her hand in my curls and lifted sharply.

"Take off my pants," she instructed. My knees waded into the muck below her, knocking over twigs and something metal underfoot. I unzipped her jeans and pulled them down.

"Come on. We don't have all night," she commanded. I took her in my mouth and wondered if she wanted a pussy. She brought her face close to mine. "You're too fast. You have to warm into it. And I forgot to kiss you. You're a lady after all."

Rough lips grazed mine. Tentative at first then wet with pride, temporary ownership through truce. Her fingers slid to down my torso and I squirmed. We kissed again with reckless force. She wasn't inside me anymore, both of her hands cradled my head with affection. I wondered what she saw in me. An escape route or something more. I always got too caught up in what other people wanted—Ash's white picket fences, Ryan's fireworks, whatever T4T royalty Max chased. What Indigo wanted was to feel something visceral. I imagined that the sex she had with most of the other girls at Herculine felt restrictive in a way. It could only be made anew so many times. Indigo slid three fingers into my ass and started working my pussy with her other hand, letting me get slick.

"I'm not going to cum today. Too much spiro," she said. "But you are."

I bit her neck hard as she dug her fingers into me.

"No hickeys," she hissed. But she bit me too.

I started cumming to the thought of the first time Ash and I ever fucked. Through my orgasm, I saw Legion's endless eyes. I screamed. Indigo lurched backward. We waited a few minutes before saying anything. Fresh tears were pooling down my cheeks.

"Are you okay?" she asked.

"No," I whispered. "No."

She moved closer, her hands getting ready to scoop me like peach ice cream, but I winced and shifted away.

"Please, no."

We sat next to each other naked and shivering under a flock of crows.

GIRLS 'R' US

I started watching Ash the same way she kept tabs on me. If she could really peer into my mind like Indigo said, I had to have some defensive edge. Maybe she was just playing with me, trying to amp up my fear and keep me away from the woman she used to love. But I had a creeping suspicion there was more to it than that.

"What was dating in New York like?" Indigo asked me at the dinner table, looking directly at me with firing squad eyes.

I was surprised she was addressing me in front of everyone. Ash sat next to me with her arm around my shoulder. Her new bitch Izzie sat perfectly composed across the table. The whole meal I'd been too busy watching Ash watching her. Esther and Elle perched next to each other slurping their broth. Somehow they were already beginning to show. Esther looked deep in thought, she stopped eating and stared at her bowl with empty eyes.

"Fine," I said and took a sip of Diet Coke and looked at the butternut squash in front of me. It was a terrible depression soup.

"And?" Indigo pushed.

Izzie giggled. I wanted to take her by the ponytail and smash her pretty porcelain face against the table until it was branded with splinters.

"I was straight for a while," I said.

"No you weren't." Elle laughed. "No way."

"Basically," I said, avoiding Indigo's gaze. "Besides Ash. I mostly dated guys in New York. I've never slept with a cis girl. I've only slept with a few other trans girls."

"Is it because you don't think we're real girls?" Izzie said.

"We're as real as a trip to Girls 'R' Us can get," I said.

"Fuck off," Ash said, lightly hitting my arm.

"I'm kidding. I think we're real. I don't like debating how real."

"Mmm," Izzie said. "Some internalized truscum transmisogyny."

"That's not what I mean."

"Then what do you mean?" Ash asked, taking over for her sexual protégée.

"Do you talk to your mom about the people you date? Does she know you're here?" Indigo asked. I looked to Ash but she was busy. She didn't even seem to be in the same room with us.

"She's pretty Christian. But I don't know, sometimes we talk about things. She got over the trans thing. More or less. We just kind of . . . moved on."

"Have you?" Izzie said. "My foster mom's in jail. She drove her car off a bridge with me and all my foster siblings inside."

The room quieted, waiting for her to go on. She purposefully slurped another spoonful of soup. The whole bad-girl routine annoyed me.

"Izzie . . ." Elle pleaded. "What the fuck happened?"

"My foster mom had a thing for 'gender-troubled' kids. She adopted, like, eight of us or something. She would march all of us to church in a nice long row. Made us iron our clothes and would burn us with it if we acted too girly, too butch, too whatever. She was *obsessed* with the Sylvia Likens case. Even drove us over to her house once. Lucky for us it wasn't that far away. My foster mom thought she could do better. Or worse. Sometimes she kept me locked in the basement for days. Made me drink my own piss." She paused and looked at me then back at her soup. It was a rotten, mushy green color. "Anyway. One day she came home and started whaling on this gay guy a few years older than me. He started fighting back for once. Then this butch girl came up from behind and knocked the wind out of her. We just all mutinied. We made her drive off that bridge at knife point. Somehow we all survived. We were ready to die though. We all told the cops the same story and she went to jail. Case closed."

Everyone was quiet for a while. Ruby lips formed a joker's smile. Ash sat down by Izzie and leaned into her while squeezing her arm.

"Fuck moms," Indigo said.

"My mom was the sweetest," Elle said. "I miss her."

I left the sad-girl soup and mommy issues to the other girls. If Ash was going to rub a burgeoning little affair in my face, hypocrite that I was, I wasn't going to watch. I came across Esther looking sullenly at the ground. I hadn't noticed her leave.

"You okay?" I asked.

She put her hands in the pockets of her white poplin dress and walked off without saying anything. Pregnancy's a bitch, I thought. Maybe she was hormonal. It seemed impossible to go through the process without some growing pains. She and Elle were so young to be mothers. How did everyone think they were going to take care of two little ones? None of them had ever been parents. Not in the real way. I bucked at the thought. It felt like internalized transphobia to acknowledge the difference. But it wasn't just about biology, it was about age. And care.

Still, I wanted Esther to be happy so that I could imagine myself happy. Maybe that was foolish. To tack my hope onto someone else's. We do it all the time though; we base our own capacity on another's. The entire project seemed outrageous. To go against God and nature to reclaim the womb. To raise kids collectively. I'd heard about studies being done in faraway countries but the reality of a trans woman having a kid with her own uterus seemed so far away. There were so many possible complications. But now I was a witness. A possible test subject. For so long I'd toyed with the possibility of being a mother, trying to break through my ambivalence. I always pushed it off, it wasn't the kind of choice I needed to make. It wasn't like I ever had a stable partner to build a home with anyway. Now I was being forced to think about the possibility again, this time with real consequences. I hadn't accomplished anything I thought I needed to before starting a family. I hadn't written a book. I hadn't gotten married. I hadn't even been proposed to. All of those were things I thought I needed to accomplish before taking care of someone else. To care required being cared for—even if by myself. When I tried to imagine myself standing over a crib I only saw an empty child's bedroom. Winnie-the-Pooh painted on the wall, a Calder mobile, yellow-and-blue building blocks scattered on a lavender-colored rug. A window with pastel linen curtains. But there was no baby, no biological ticking clock. Not really. Just one day after another going down the drain.

It was no longer a surprise when demons showed up to Sunday service. After Martha gave an update about finances and Mira lectured us about Wi-Fi usage, Ash took the stage.

"I don't want to give out homework and I don't want to call anyone out, but I will assign *The Ethical Slut* if I have to," Ash said.

The joke seemed pointed, but I thought she should try to give it a read first. Everyone liked to talk a big game about preventing hurt without looking in the mirror. Monogamy was a shackle Ash toyed with, but her rules were never explicit. I did actually want to be someone's possession though. Every new lover was an opportunity to be worn. But each time I was tried on, I was eventually discarded. A younger, prettier, more passing model was never far behind. Scanning the pews, I located Indigo sitting next to the Hot Butch. Both of them were wearing wifebeaters that accentuated their hard nipples. I had never been a cheater. I told myself the circumstances were different at Herculine. All is fair in love and demonology.

"Now for an update on our two radiant pregnant ladies," Ash said. Elle and Esther were seated near her, handmaidens of Herculine. Elle was beaming but Esther seemed nervous as they listened to the service. "Dagon has blessed us with two children. We will welcome them and build an altar to our lord. Someone who won't ever fail us. Now our glowing mothers-to-be are going to say a few words."

Elle opened her mouth to speak but Esther cut her off.

"I don't want it!" she screamed.

The air turned cool. I was standing right next to the fiery altar at the front of the room, but it did not warm my bones, it felt wet behind me. I searched for Indigo for some indication of what was to come. Esther was shaking. She'd seemed so calm and collected just moments ago. I was surprised to see her so out of sorts. Suddenly, four girls I didn't know very well joined in her chorus of screaming. The green translucent bug demon crawled between them as they scattered. Its body was still not wholly solid and it glittered in the light like a gem.

"Oh Dagon," Ash said. She looked vacant, like kindling for the great fire. "Lord of the Deep." She looked vacant when she let a demon take over. Like Cassandra—just a vessel for knowledge. Her eyes like two orbs full of lies.

I will devour . . . every one of you . . . who does not appreciate my gifts . . .

One of Dagon's many green antennae slowly swept the room. The demon came across Esther and dug into her belly with military-like precision.

Esther screamed. The others watched in horror as the parasitic limb dug through Esther's stomach. We could see where it bulged, worming through her in search of the fetus. I wondered how far along she was. Esther writhed in pain until Dagon used two other antennae to pin her to the ground. No one moved to help. Elle was tearing up. Ash still looked blank. I realized I was getting used to the noise. Surely Esther's screams alone hit an insane decibel, but everything sounded oddly muted. The sound no longer registered as it once did.

Whores, whores, ungrateful girls, evil girls. Stupid, stupid girls. You will never be women.

When the antennae retracted, black mud puddled underneath Esther. She let out a singular sob and then looked down. She struggled to get up, blood drooling down her leg and green gunk splattered across the hem of her yellow frock and her toes. She managed to walk back to the pews before collapsing on the ground. The first trans-girl abortion. We all silently contemplated. The effigy next to Ash was vibrating. Indigo stood next to me, quiver at her side, bow on her back.

"Sometimes the demons get cagey. I'm guessing it didn't like little Esther's confession," she told me.

"I didn't know she felt that way," I said.

Ash's eyes were white. Esther sobbed on the floor as Elle knelt to help her. Dagon unsheathed more tendrils and launched them in all directions. They pierced the sides of the building like an insect tree sprouting from between the pews. Next the beast took aim at the soft wood, breaking it apart.

"We should get out," I said.

"No," Indigo said.

Ash still stood next to the effigy, murmuring in Latin, as Izzie cowered nearby, her eyes wide with fear. Mira, Martha, and a few other girls huddled around Esther, as if able to protect her. I put my odds for survival on the girls who ran. Dagon's tendrils hovered in the air. The room was silent for a minute. Then more screaming erupted as Dagon swept a few girls off the ground, twisting their bodies like strawberry caps in its steely grip. Natalie's body hit the floor first. We could all hear her bones crunching. I looked away. I did not want to see ivory bone poking through Gushers-red muscle.

"What did she do?" I heard Izzie's squeaky voice ask.

The three remaining girls in Dagon's grasp rained down from the sky as the translucent bug demon took flight through the roof, leaving the survivors to sort out the carnage ourselves. Everyone rushed toward the wounded girls. Indigo and I exchanged glances.

"Meet me at the trailhead in two hours, if you can," she said, before turning to help Esther.

I couldn't stop staring at Natalie's lifeless, broken body. A few traumatized girls walked out in silence. I slipped into the crowd behind Elle. She held her stomach as we walked down the two steps and toward her cabin.

An hour and a half later, I came across a solemn gathering of defectors at the top of a dense wooded incline. Indigo, Martha, and two other girls sat on a log, whispering about the massacre. Down the hill, the camp was still alight. No one wanted to go to bed just yet.

"I can't believe Natalie died . . ." Martha said. There were tears in her eyes. I wanted to put my hand on hers but resisted the impulse.

"We could be next," the One with the Pink Hair added.

"She wasn't even in our group," Indigo said. "The other girls were just casualties too, I don't think this was about us."

"Next time it might be," the One with the Pink Hair countered.

"We have to get out," Indigo said. "And soon."

She was staring right at me, waiting for me to pledge fealty.

"How do you propose we do that?" I asked.

"We'll have to use our tethers," Indigo said.

"Are you kidding me? Did we witness the same thing? That demon just bled that girl out for wanting an abortion," I said. I had risen to my feet, surprised at how good it felt to talk back to someone, to speak in anger, even if it wasn't directed at the person I was most furious at.

"Don't be a fucking smart-ass," Martha yelled. "They didn't punish Natalie because Esther wanted an abortion."

"Then why did she die?" I asked. "If that's how they treat the girls they like, then how the hell do you think we're going get out of here?"

"Nihilism isn't going to help," Indigo said. She stood up to level with me, face-to-face. I sat back down.

"People are dead. That seems like punishment to me," I said.

"I hardly think demons care about abortion one way or the other," the Hot Butch said, staring me down.

"We're getting off track. You're the only one not yet tethered. You have the best chance of leading us out of here."

"*Leading?*" I pushed. My voice squeaked. "How do you suggest that I get us out of whatever"—I motioned furiously—"demonic force field is around us?"

"Let me worry about that for now. I have some ideas. We'll have to wait a few days before we meet again. Then we can go over the details."

She shot me a flirtatious look as I looked down at the ground and let my face go numb. We staggered our exits. I left last, slowly hiking back down the hill toward the lights.

When I got back to Ash's house, I caught a flustered, nude Izzie hastily tying a bathrobe around her waist as she walked out the front door. She stopped when she saw me. I stared at her untrimmed bush.

"Hi," she said.

"Hi."

"I'd better go."

"Okay," I said.

Izzie scampered off, desperately holding the corners of the bathrobe to her body.

Quietly, I made my way into our cabin. Her cabin, really.

"Ash?"

She was sitting on the ground in a blue bathrobe smoking a Capri. Her hair was bundled up atop her head, mousy strands falling next to her cheeks.

I sat down a few feet away and held my knees in close.

"Hey."

"Hey," she said quietly, almost as if it wasn't me in the room with her and she was talking to a ghost.

"Why was Izzie in here?"

Ash shrugged.

"Just talking?" I suggested.

"Just talking."

"Okay," I said.

"It's nothing," Ash said. "You just keep pulling away."

"Why don't we run away together? Can't we leave this place and start over?"

"It's too late. Everything's in motion."

"What's in motion? The tethering? Can't . . . Can't we get out of it?"

She turned toward me and I saw there were tears in her eyes for the first time since I'd arrived. She could still feel something. She was in there.

"No. You can't get out of it."

I pulled her in and kissed her hard on the lips. I had come seeking reassurance and answers but there I was trying to make her feel okay about everything she'd done to me. Funny how that happened. She nuzzled her head against my breast as I tried to think about what to do next. Confrontation with her was always like watching a slow-burning moth. So beautifully tender I didn't know what to do but stop and watch the embers in the moonlight.

DON'T LEAVE THE HOUSE

The next death happened with less fanfare. Two days later we found the Hot Butch from Indigo's rebellion, dead in her bed after she didn't come out for breakfast, lunch, or dinner. Indigo told me that I was too delicate to see the body. I took her word for it after seeing Natalie. Apparently, the girl's death didn't stink of the supernatural. Indigo wondered if Ash was onto us. Paranoid, she started creating hand signs for us to flash at one another. No notes, no words. Not unless we were far enough away from the camp. When we walked past each other, we kept our distance, even as I filled with perverse desire. I kept imagining our night in the woods and longed to fuck myself. I couldn't even take out my sexual frustrations on Ash—I was terrified that if she and I fucked, she would choke me a few seconds too long.

"What's wrong?" she kept asking as if we could have an honest conversation.

The small peace that had been established in Herculine was gone. No one felt safe. Girls whispered in corners. On my way to breakfast, a girl with a septum piercing shot me a death glare. She, like many others, thought it was my fault, that I was a harbinger of death. I felt something wet on the back of my leg and realized that she'd spit on me. Great.

"Fuck off," I muttered under my breath.

"Excuse me?" the girl huffed, turning around to face me.

I didn't say anything, just stared back at her blankly. Indigo started walking over to us, but I just wanted to be left alone and de-escalate the situation myself. I motioned for her to stand down, and the girl continued along her way.

The Hot Butch's death scared me too, but no one cared about my fear. I was expendable, I was the one in the wrong. Both the other girls in Indigo's clique and the ones on Ash's side treated me like a social pariah and looked at me weird if I tried to sit with them at mealtimes. I grabbed a piece of toast and headed for the door. Elle smiled at me as I passed her on my way out. Elle was one of the few who remained friendly with me, her maternal glow expanding like a ballooning leech. The thin ache I'd once felt for motherhood was rotting as I considered that the demons were artificially shaping her emotions. The daily joy she made out of being pregnant was cursed. Even Ash grew increasingly distant—sometimes when I woke up she was already out for the day. Or maybe she was just waking up in Izzie's bed. I didn't understand how someone who'd attempted murder-suicide was more appealing than me.

Legion seemed to be playing the long game, suggesting that he wasn't worried that I would actually manage to escape. I didn't really feel like there was anywhere to escape *to*. Even if I got away from Ash—which I still felt conflicted about—Legion would be waiting. It wasn't like the demons first appeared to me when I'd arrived at Herculine. I'd always been haunted. He was patiently taking his time tethering to me, waiting until I was at my lowest. I wasn't sure how much lower I could go.

Indigo wanted to meet up and talk about her friend's death. I kept blowing her off. I wasn't particularly close to the butch who'd died or Natalie. But in a matter of days, our numbers dwindled from twenty to fifteen. I felt like I should've felt sorrow but instead I felt dead, nauseated twenty-four seven. Indigo's voice rang in my mind, repeating the same messages about how little time we had, how Ash was going to discard me, how Legion was going to bind to me and I wouldn't be strong enough to resist. Even if we sailed out of Herculine into the great big wide world together, Indigo did not seem like the kind of woman I would want to build a house with. But she was good at fucking. And she was right, Ash did not take full advantage of my body. Especially after Izzie showed up. Maybe Izzie got the real sex. I was supposed to be having good sex. The earth-shattering, spiritual kind that brought me back to life and then cast me out into the wilderness with a new lease on life. I still hoped that I was the one she really needed. The one she would return to again and again. Wishful thinking had never saved me before, but there was always a chance to try again.

I decided to walk along the river for a while. Leaves fell into the water, following the current like me. I missed being near the ocean in New York—not that I actually visited it all that often. I missed taking walks from Fourteenth Street to Central Park, wearing out the soles of my shoes and praying that with one more cup of bodega coffee I would be able to solve my emotional problems. I always just wanted love. Too bad I looked for it in foxholes. I wanted the dangerous love built on long-distance plane rides, trauma, and failed girlhood. I thought about Joni Mitchell singing about danger and repetition after leaving her lover at a truck stop and driving cross-country in disguise. I hummed the lyrics for the hundredth time, over someone else I felt could be the one to tie me up in white lace. For years in therapy I had spit out the Ouroboros of my love life. The opposite of a rainbow. That's what I'd followed across the Midwest. I shouldn't have left New York. Leaving one hell for another is never a good idea. Don't leave the house. Stay put. Weather ennui. I was striving to learn a lesson without having finished the journey. Therapized beyond belief.

I took off my boots and plopped my feet into the river with two small splashes though it was far too cold. Jesus help me. I felt the words welling up inside me. The prayers my grandma had taught me resurfacing, tokens against obliteration. Branches swayed above me in the breeze. I put my hands in my coat pockets and considered smoking another cigarette but I'd forgotten my lighter. After a few restless moments I got out, put my shoes back on, and continued wandering into the woods. The trees tangled thick around me, evergreens and notched birches. Mist shrouded the path in front. I decided to find the small briar patch that Indigo had told me about. Behind a crumbling wall and a dense thicket lay some wild berries and clover. It always made me think of children's storybooks. I would pick some forbidden fruit. I wound my way through the maze of peeling bark and crunching leaves.

There was no gate on the briar patch and the wall was too desecrated to keep anyone in or out. I lifted one leg then the other. Tall girl. I hated it when cis people reminded me that I was tall. Once, a woman I had only ever talked to on the phone told me that I was taller than she'd expected when she finally met me in person. I was proud of that. My boss said she was probably humoring me. I made a low-grade snipe about her Elizabeth Warren sticker.

I felt demonic logic clouding my mind, just being in Herculine affected my brain. God wasn't going to save me. I could beg on my knees, sweat, drive a tent peg through the head of my enemy. Serve Ash's head on a platter. But I didn't want to do any of that. If someone else told me they'd had to kill to get out of such a position I would have forgiven them. I wasn't sure I would allow myself the same luxury. Besides, it could've been what Legion wanted, for me to lose my soul. It occurred to me he could've been listening in on my thoughts. I took a deep breath and wormed my way through the thorns, letting nettles collect on my skin. Cuts formed quickly, and by the time I was in the middle of the secret garden, I looked like a lesser Saint Sebastian.

All through my childhood, Revelation was read aloud at night. My mom and grandma watched animated Christmas specials obsessively. In our corner of the country, we never separated the church from the state. Even if such a country was out there that truly followed that doctrine, it'd be haunted by the morality of nationalism. When my dad ran out on us, he left a thick stack of spiritual-warfare books behind. Exorcisms, demonology, Wiccan practices. He scrutinized the Satanic Panic of the 1980s and '90s as a way of understanding the rot corrupting our nation. Things that went bump in the night required a supernatural explanation. All the infamous murderers, unexplained phenomena, and shows like *The X-Files* were fodder for this theory. Christians love a unifying theory. The trouble was, he was right about something. Demons were real. I stopped walking and laughed out loud. It was insane! I was insane! I had grown up in a world of nightmares and now they were going to eat me alive. I tried to remember how the paranormal investigators in my dad's books made it out. Garlic wasn't going to cut it. I wondered if I needed the strength of prayer warriors. It never made sense to me why God would be a punisher. I could believe that He was distant or that He was kind, but a vengeful God was difficult to integrate into the world as I knew it. Or maybe I just didn't want to. Christianity asked me to be good, but good was such a fragile thing. I worried that I'd mapped those values onto my politics. I believed that if I believed I was worthy then I would be. But I didn't. I made lists of my faults.

The thistle in front of me was worn down. Clearly someone else had been here before me. I decided it didn't matter and kept walking. It was a very meditative little spot. I found a little rock surrounded by weeds and sat down.

As I listened to a robin tweeting overhead, I thought about Mary Oliver running around the woods with her notebook and her lover after all the abuse. She stopped dragging her body through the desert to repent. The veil was torn open. I thought about when Assata escaped prison. An empire had failed in its task of stripping her autonomy.

"I decided," Assata said.

Is transcendence enough?

What is enough?

An action?

A tendency?

A belief?

A vision?

A hope not seen?

Or, is it faith? Let's read about faith from Saint Paul. A letter to Jerusalem: "Now faith is the substance of things hoped for, the evidence of things not seen." Or perhaps, "Now *enough* is the substance of things hoped for, the evidence of things not seen."

I remembered the high school teacher who gave me a book that said hell wasn't real, that literary studies could trace the way hell evolved from a word for the town dump. A metaphor turned into a physical location, the danger of speaking with anaphora. Just tell me the facts. The answer of how to escape the ethics of tautology, of Christianity's self-affirming imperialism—it is because it is—God is because God is—is that you have to
—as Mary and Assata did—

walk away.

Love is patient, love is kind, it does not envy, it does not boast, it is not proud, it does not dishonor others, it is not self-seeking, love does not delight in evil but rejoices in the truth . . . love never fails.

Love is not a fire, but a river, a flow, an ease. I remember when loving Ash felt like a river. I remember when love was enough. I remember when love will be enough again.

I got up and started walking back toward the gate when something caught my eye. On the far side of the thicket was a cave. A small mound of limestone with a large opening, jagged with weeds and dust. Maybe a bear lived there. My whole life I kept trying to walk away and there I was, still walking straight into the lion's den. I had two poles to walk away from—both equally perilous. On one side, a God with a sadistic streak, on the other demons with nefarious charm. Resisting the idea of a new face, tits, and a pussy was still a little difficult, even after all the horrors I'd seen.

In the depths of the cave a single red light blinked at me. I felt the growing mist around me seething with humidity as the wind picked up. The outline of a demon was faintly visible. I could see his slime starting to coat the walls of the cave, drawing me toward him with a hypnotic spell. It was not Legion, but I still did not want him in my space. I wanted to breathe deeply and feel home again.

"Leave," another voice firmly called through the ether.

I couldn't tell where this second voice was coming from. The demon started to walk toward me. I rushed out of the briar patch, hurdling over the wall. I didn't look back. Nothing reached out to grab my shoulder, no spidery leg or razor-sharp claw. With every step I took, I refused to turn back, no matter what I heard behind me. The sounds slowly muted as I carried on.

When I reached the river I stopped to catch my breath, sighing deeply. I pondered what exactly I would do if I ever made it back to New York. A sword would have been nice to have on hand. Excalibur maybe.

NETTLES

The next morning I went to check on my car again. I didn't expect it to work, but I was devastated to find it had been all but destroyed. Someone had slashed all four wheels and pummeled the motor with a hammer.

"What's wrong?" Ash said. She wrapped her hands around my waist in reassurance.

"Look for yourself," I said.

"Your demon must be getting ready to come," she said. I turned around to face her, flaring with rage, until I saw her solemn face. She looked worried. "I can help you. Tethering isn't easy but I can help you prepare."

"How?"

Elle waddled over, her belly plump and smooth, poking out from underneath a sweater.

"Maternity clothes from an Indiana Goodwill. Not as good a selection as I would've thought." Elle sucked on a green Popsicle and glanced at my car. "That sucks."

"Yeah."

I turned away from the small group gathered around the ruins of my car. I brushed Ash off. Even before I was out of view they had already started talking about me. The bonfire and I kept each other company. For the past week, everyone worked to keep the flame in the middle of the cabins going all day and all night. I enjoyed the warmth in the late September mornings.

Indigo still wanted to make a break for it. We were finally supposed to meet later that night to talk it over. Make a detailed plan, gather supplies in an unused shed. Sometimes she tried to hold my hand when Ash wasn't looking. Her love was driven by pessimistic lust. I think the one time we fucked had felt like freedom to her.

I heard a revving noise down the dirt road that led away from camp. Someone on a motorcycle was speeding toward Herculine. For a minute I worried it was Legion finally coming for me. I ran back to my broken car where the gravel met cattails. The red motorcycle slowed. When it came to a complete stop, the cyclist took off her helmet and let two small ponytails tumble out on either side of her face. A little angel doll. Hazel, I realized. I felt guilty almost immediately, this wasn't going to end well for anyone.

Indigo and her defector crew crawled out to see who the new girl was. The final girl. Ash was still milling around by my car, smiling in a pink bra and jeans. I never noticed how hot Hazel was until I saw her up against our ragtag cult. She was a knockout even without surgical intervention. With, she'd be the most annoying girl of all time. Izzie ran up to Ash's side. I couldn't see any of the girls carrying weapons, but I knew that there were demons all around us, ready to materialize in an instant. Leaving was not going to be an easy maneuver.

"Well, well, well," Hazel said. She was smiling. I loved her for smiling. "I found you. We've all been worried sick. You haven't returned anyone's calls in quite a while."

"Service," I mumbled, running up to hug her.

"I'd like to meet everyone but . . ." She looked around at the gaggle of girls staring blankly at her. "We should head out soon."

"I've heard so much about you," Ash said, striding over. "I'm Ash."

Hazel shot me an uneasy look. Indigo awkwardly stamped a dandelion under her boot.

"Hello," Hazel said.

"Welcome to Herculine," Ash said. She looked troubled by this development, probably thinking about how Hazel's arrival could undo all her hard work. I wondered if she was trying to peer into my mind so she could uncover my next move.

"Thanks."

Elle suckled the last of her Popsicle and threw the stick on the ground. Hazel was eying her with wonder. I could see her disbelief rubbing elbows with fear. For once she was a little out of her depth.

"Why are you so sure she wants to leave?" Elle asked. Her eyes were almost completely dead. They looked like Ash's right before she'd pierced my heart with something I didn't even realize I wanted. "I feel like she's been having an okay time."

Hazel smiled. "I'm sure she has. Maybe she'll come back, if she wants."

"Were you two . . . involved?" Ash asked.

We both burst out laughing.

"No," Hazel said. "I'd never fuck you. No offense."

"Fuck you," I said. "C'mon, let's go on a little walk,"

"I do need to stretch my legs for a second," Hazel replied.

"You should at least stay for lunch," Ash yelled after us as we strolled off. "We want to get to know you better!" She almost sounded desperate.

"She's been calling you honeysuckle?" Hazel asked. Her pupils danced.

"Yeah," I said.

"Then I'll start calling you nettles. A counterbalance."

"I'm glad you came," I said. "But also I hate that you're here."

"Then it's just like always," Hazel said.

I tried to explain the last few weeks to her but failed, stammering incoherently. Nothing I said made much sense and I could tell she was struggling to believe me. Phantoms and insect demons weren't a part of her lexicon.

"Tell me why I shouldn't take you straight to the psych ward?" Hazel asked. It landed somewhere between a joke and a threat.

"I'm mad, sure, but I don't hallucinate."

"No time like the present to sta—"

"Shut up, Hazel. This place is dangerous. Getting out of here won't be that easy," I said.

"Oh, come on."

"They wrecked my car."

"Then we should just get on my bike and leave right now."

"When did you get your license anyway?"

"I didn't. When I got to L.A. some girl I fucked a few times taught me how to ride and stay alive."

"Staying alive sounds good."

"It's warmer in L.A.," Hazel said. "Fewer weeds too."

"It's called nature," I said. We grazed our hands over the moss and sat in silence. She was uneasy. I was still in shock. "Did you end up getting that show? Are you going to be the trans Carrie Bradshaw?"

"No. They went with some girl who's been on hormones since she was, like, twelve. A model. She's really pretty."

Apparently, Hazel went on, the Famous Trans-Girl Actress had also been considered for the role but was ultimately turned away for being too old. She would play a bit part instead, introducing the new young thing to an infamous chaser.

"Isn't it supposed to be reality television?"

Hazel gave me a look and pivoted to some non sequitur about poison ivy and itchy pussy.

"Hey, that one girl . . ." Hazel trailed off, but I knew she meant Elle. "Is she . . . ?"

"Pregnant," I said.

"No way."

"She is."

"Ash seems like a fucking cunt," Hazel said without missing a beat.

"She wasn't always."

How many sides can a person have? How often are all of them the worst? The worst part about a breakup, especially a drawn-out one, was slowly watching yourself tear someone you loved into a thousand tiny little pieces. Everything you loved about them minimized, every sin put under a magnifying glass. Proportions reflected through a fun house mirror. Worse, your friends tell you everything they hated about them.

"She's not very pretty," Hazel said. I didn't say anything. We let the silence of the forest swallow her words whole. "Is that smoke?"

We both stared at Herculine stretching out below us. A pillar of smoke drifted up from the chapel. It was big enough that it would soon attract attention. Every cult fell one way or another.

When we reached the commune, an awful shriek hollowed our stomachs. Elle was in labor. I could tell by the way her voice had turned wolfish. The scream of a chronic smoker. We walked farther into camp. What we'd thought was a column of smoke from farther away was a demon turning corporeal above the chapel.

It was Legion, shifting onto our plane. Well. It had to happen sooner or later.

MOUTH'S CRADLE

Evil is just as patient as love. It bends the arc of the universe with steady hands.

The air was thick with smog and an endless swarm of flies. I couldn't get warm and I couldn't cool down. Hazel managed to stay by my side in the chaos. We were standing behind Ash's cabin. Girls ran around in a flurry. In the distance we saw something explode. Hazel made the connection first.

"My motorcycle!"

Our options were dwindling. I tried to crane my neck to find Indigo or one of the other defectors to quickly organize a plan, but I couldn't make out much. Izzie was headed for the main hall. She was carrying a bucket of water and a tiny yellow sponge. That didn't bode well. I motioned for Hazel to follow me.

"You really want to go into the thick of it?"

"What else are we gonna do?"

"I don't know, try to hot-wire one of their cars?"

"Where'd you learn how to do that?"

"Nora." Hazel smirked.

"Just fucking date her already."

I watched her run toward the edge of Herculine, her clothes hounded by the wind. Girlhood is dressing slutty in cold weather. Maybe womanhood too.

The outside of the hall was buzzing with grasshoppers. I entered slowly. Blood gushed over the floorboards. Elle was laid out underneath the effigy I'd faced dozens of times before, but now there was another beside it. A few girls were screaming in the pews. Elle's child was clearly not human, but I couldn't get a real look at the thing. The strange babe scampered back and forth across the floor. Dagon was hovering somewhere between our realm and another, his exoskeleton glittering in the haze. The roof of the chapel was gone. Leaving not even a stray shingle behind. In the smoky sky, the body of Legion gathered corporeal form. By the time I got to Elle she was moaning unintelligibly.

"What's going on?"

Elle wasn't going to be saying much, I realized as I surveyed her injuries. Esther and Izzie sprung up from behind a ripped-up pew.

"Ash said it's time," Izzie said, struggling to get the words out calmly.

"What does that mean?" I asked. "We were only gone for a few hours."

"She summoned Asmodeus," Izzie said. Her teeth were chattering. "As soon as you left, she called us in for a surprise meeting."

Apparently, Ash tied up the One with the Pink Hair, suspecting her of being a defector like the Hot Butch. I looked again at the second figure at the front of the chapel, and sure enough, it was the girl's body, fashioned into a morbid scarecrow. A corpse. There wasn't much left of the girl, her flesh was torn off in strips as if something had mauled her. I barely recognized her as the same girl I'd once asked to pass me the oatmeal at breakfast. Her head was nowhere in sight, though a few frizzy pink strands of her hair remained. I had to look away after spotting her entrails snaking across the floor. Izzie had already emptied her stomach a few feet away. I couldn't blame her. The whole sight was nauseating. I could feel the wind leaving my body. There were no lines left to cross. The stench alone was enough to signal the irredeemability of Ash's actions. I spit up some bile and blinked a few times to compose myself. Debris fell from the ceiling. I wondered how many other girls were hiding inside the room.

"I get the gist," I said. "Where's Ash now?"

Izzie and Esther looked at me like I was crazy.

"Where is she?" I barked.

"I don't know. Everyone scattered after the sacrifice," Izzie whispered. "Then Dagon came and Elle went into labor."

"And the thing above us?"

"I don't know."

"Get as many of the girls as you can and take them far away from here," I instructed.

"Fuck off," Izzie said, gaining steam. I wasn't Ash's pet anymore. I held no sway.

"Elle needs help. At least get her out of here," I said.

Elle moaned beside us, crimson dripping from her body and crystallizing like wax. A pumping green umbilical cord slithered next to her. Izzie and Esther slowly helped Elle up, distributing her weight between the two of them. They were inching their way toward the door when they caught Dagon's notice. Tiny sharp antennae burst forth from his abdomen like daggers and pierced the walls.

"Leave her."

Izzie and Esther let Elle drop like a rock. She screamed in pain.

"Go," I mouthed. They inched toward the door before breaking out in a full sprint once they realized that Dagon wasn't planning to pursue them—Elle was his primary interest.

"Elle. Elle, stay with me," I cooed, squatting down to hold her close to me.

"It crawled out of me," Elle said. "It was so cold."

"You're okay," I said. "It's going to be okay. You've just lost a little blood."

"Get me out of here. Get me out!" she screamed. "I don't want to be here anymore. I wanna go home."

"Okay, okay. Let's get you home."

Too bad I didn't have any holy oil with me. Still, I wasn't sure that Christian mystic relics would do much against this nightmare. I thought about charging the beast kamikaze style. Trannies are not supposed to make jokes about killing ourselves. But we all know, even good trannies go to hell.

The tendrils lashed against the walls as soon as I got to my feet. In retrospect, I'm not sure what came over me other than my brush with death made me realize that living could be nice. There were still some things I wanted to do. I'd barely left the country. I'd never taken a dance class or kissed a celebrity or written a best-selling memoir. That, and spite. I did not want to die in my ex-girlfriend's lesbian utopia. I wanted to die in the hands of someone who loved me.

"I'm going now," I declared.

Elle's demon baby surfaced from beneath the floorboards. A little grasshopper bobblehead atop a human body covered in flaking scabs. The child was already three feet tall. Two pairs of translucent wings hung from the little beast's back as it scampered across the room toward us—mandible first. The Antichrist was a lot smaller than I'd expected. I used my body to block Elle's, trying my best to keep the thing away from us. The bug child crawled all over me, biting my back and arms. There were precious few weapons in the chapel. No crucifixes that could be used to masturbate with or stab a demonic pest.

The original effigy, however, was hoisted up on a metal pole. Whatever artistic merit Ash was going for, it looked like shit. More arts and crafts than night terror. Still, I prayed the pole would be sharp enough to pierce an otherworldly exoskeleton. I shook the insect off my back and scrambled to yank the wannabe pagan fixtures off the pole, tossing aside the birdlike woman and her hazmat suit. I drew it up like Excalibur and ran toward the little demon child. I could feel Dagon exploiting my emotions. But for once, I saw through it. It wasn't quite CBT rewriting-the-narrative bullshit. I just cussed him out, letting my anger and vitriol drown out his.

I missed.

The child's beady eyes stared mockingly at me. They looked so empty. A tendril drilled into the floor behind me as I jumped over the remnants of a broken pew. The little bitch was so fast. My back bloomed with pain. The babe had scratched me with its pincer, leaving behind a long streak of blood. I caught a glimpse of myself in a shattered mirror. My shirt fell in tatters at my waist, exposing my white bra, now brown with blood and grime. I had scratches and dust all over my stomach. And I really should've put my hair up before running in to save anyone.

I ran to one of the bookshelves and waited for the bug to come get me. Death wish or bust. The child scuttled toward me, flanked by Dagon's swirling limbs. With the last remaining ounce of my strength, I pulled the heavy bookcase down over us. Trapping the child, the tendrils, and me underneath its massive weight. The child emitted a squelch like a stomped cockroach. Dagon screamed in agony, and I wondered if perhaps it felt sorrow as well. I yelped in pain, struggling to crawl out from under the shelf. I could feel the nasty violet bruise forming on my back as I pushed myself free and retrieved the pole, stabbing the bug demon a few times for good measure. I was out of breath when I finally grabbed Elle and started dragging her out of the chapel. Behind us, I could feel the crusty core of Legion manifesting.

The cabins were wrecked. Windows broken, roofs caved in. As we struggled across the commune, we saw the carnage. Some belonged to girls I'd never talked to, their bodies disfigured and burned by campfire. Martha's figure was twisted into an impossible configuration, limbs akimbo, and from a distance, I spotted Izzie, impaled by one of Dagon's tendrils. Straight through the left lung. Instantaneous. At least, I hoped so. Before I thought that perhaps the demons would be content with regaining control, but if a loyalist like Izzie was up for grabs, I was surely not far down the line.

Indigo and Ash were yelling at each other, surrounded by the remaining survivors. Everyone was losing it. As I drew closer, I noticed that Ash was wearing my Metallica tee. Very apocalypse chic. My ex-girlfriend, the Antichrist. Mira rushed over and helped me lower Elle to the ground. Indigo and Ash paused their argument and moved toward me with icy precision.

"Is she okay?" Mira asked.

"Maybe," I said. "I'm not sure."

"That could've been me," Esther sighed.

"Where's Hazel?" I asked, turning to Indigo.

"I don't know, I didn't see you two get back," she said.

"We have to find her."

"There's no time," Indigo said. "Now's our chance. We have to make a break for it."

"You're not leaving," Ash said. Her voice didn't sound different exactly, but there was an off note in nearly every consonant, like she was relearning how to speak. "This is it. This is what we've waited for. Legion has come to claim you. You're ready."

"I'm going to find Hazel," I said, staring Indigo in the face. I etched her slate eyes in my mind. "Just get Elle out of here."

"So fiery all of a sudden," Ash said. Her eyes were fully dilated.

Indigo looked around at the other girls. Mira, Ether, and three others awkwardly moved toward her.

"I really think you should come with us," Indigo said, her hand on my shoulder.

"You're very sweet," I said curtly, "but I don't want to be your little housewife right now, I want to save my friend."

"That's not . . . We're not even—"

"Just get them out," I said.

Indigo took those who wanted to go and departed the commune into the dark woods. The chaos offered a better chance for escaping the commune. With Dagon weakened, they might stand a chance. Or at least find the nearest main road and get a ride to the hospital. Maybe once one of the girls was untethered it would be easier for the others. Indigo might be able to finally be free of Hecate. I wasn't sure if they'd make it but understood their impulse to try. When they were out of sight, Ash turned her gaze back to me.

"I think," Ash said, letting her fingers trace my back, "that Hazel is already with Legion."

I sighed and looked at the smog obscuring the chapel.

"Well then, let's go back into the demon den."

ALL GOOD TRANNIES GO TO HELL

Ash and her final girls marched me to the chapel. Dagon was no longer a swirling mass of thorned appendages, he wasn't hovering above the ground or shimmering in luminescent shades of green. He didn't even look alive.

"What happened?"

"Elle must have gotten untethered somehow," Ash said. "Dagon lost his earthly host. Now envy spreads."

"Why didn't he kill us when he had the chance?"

"Oh, babe," she said with a grin. "You're marked VIP. At least until you get claimed. As for Elle, I suppose she'd fulfilled her purpose."

Her tone had completely changed ever since Hazel arrived. No more sweetness. No more honeysuckle.

I walked over to the effigy and found the demon child's carcass.

"The little fucker in question," I said. Ash tucked a strand of hair behind her ear. Books that had once carefully lined the walls were lying in tatters amid overturned candles and blood-soaked shards of glass. A stray hymnal lay open beside Ash's feet. "Well? What now? I assume you can't usher in the end days without the demon babe."

I was no longer in my body. I wished I was at home, enjoying a shower Diet Coke. Ash moved toward me and tried to put her hands on my waist. I backed away from her until I was cornered against the burnt scarecrow, the poor girl's flesh still held in place as an offering.

"Sweet girl," Ash purred. Ash was stalling. The real apocalypse hadn't yet begun. I hadn't foiled anything by getting Elle out. "You're in heaven and you can't even see it."

"Strange vision of heaven you have, babe."

Nicknames were weapons. Just like every normal breakup, things that were once endearing became signposts of bitterness.

Darkness gathered above as the girls around me began to shake. Ash jumped on top of me, forcing me to the ground. Her hands gripped my hips, her hair wet with sweat. Regret was sexy. Pussy from the girl sending you straight to hell.

"Don't you want me one more time?"

"No," I said.

"I don't believe that. Remember that time we fucked in the bathroom? Right before I got my pussy? This could be just like that."

"Well, except now you're running a death cult and being controlled by an actual demon," I said. "Where is he anyway?"

"Ah, you want me to summon Asmodeus, our Lord of Lust?" she said like she was teasing but I knew she was serious.

I knew letting her bring in reinforcements was a bad idea, but it was the only one I had. Maybe if I went all the way in I could get all the way out.

"Fine. If you don't want one last fuck before we go through with it . . ." Ash stepped back and extended her pale arms into the air once again. We all looked up. Legion's pillar of smoke was materializing arms.

Chants of Latin filled the room. Hopefully the others really got away. As Ash continued to summon the undead, I felt a tear drying on my cheek. Part of me wanted to rip her head from her body and snap it in half like the twig she was. The other part of me wanted her to snap out of it and talk to me like she used to when we were younger.

"Asmodeus! Hear me. Come into the realm of the living for the doubtful. Join your Kings, Legion and Dagon. Summon the Seven Lords of Hell!" Such strong words from a weak woman. A woman too cowardly to initiate a real breakup, even over text. For a moment I wondered what I ever missed about her.

Lying in bed in the morning listening to the parrots in Oakland. I missed that.

Crying on her shoulder telling her something obscene my mom would say back in college.

Sitting with our feet in the river gossiping about who was fucking whom. That too.

Sharing peanut butter sandwiches in her run-down kitchen while watching black-and-white reruns and drinking the cheapest vodka we could find.

Singing Joni Mitchell and driving through the woods.

I missed all of it.

She looked sallow in the hellfire. Like a withering corpse.

Then I saw him. He had three heads. The head of a man, a sheep, and a bull. Dragon wings sprang from his back, poking through ebony and indigo scales. Fire erupted around him as he ascended onto our realm. Mira screamed first. The rest of us followed suit. This wasn't like Dagon flickering into the chapel, this was a full-fledged assault. I hadn't prepared for something so corporeal.

"Half-breeds . . ." the demon hissed hoarsely. "We are so patient in bringing you down to the world below."

Ash walked over to me, her perfect, all-American red lips pursed in a slight smile.

"Why are you doing this?" I asked, more sternly than before.

"Asmodeus is hungry," Ash replied. "The demons need offerings in order to maintain order. If I want my freedom, my power, I have to give them what they want."

"They're going to eat us?"

"No, not really. Just your souls," she said. The deal got worse and worse as time went on. Autonomy didn't seem on the table for anyone but Ash.

"Has it all been a fucking joke to you? Just preying on my feelings?"

"No," Ash said without elaborating.

Mira and the other girls were backing off. Ash smiled. Her face wrinkled as her eyes lit up.

"It's different for me. I'm not tethered. In that way, Asmodeus is both partner and master."

My allegiance had wavered long before then, but in that moment, my sorrow became a blade.

"I'm guessing the other girls don't have such a good deal," I hissed.

"No," Ash said. "Not exactly. But I need the extra strength to bring new girls in. To help them escape their abusers. To protect them while they're here. I have to work harder than anyone.

They all trade in little pieces of their souls for surgeries or whatever. I have to do my tasks first. And actually, once you're tethered, I'll finally get my own womb."

I remembered the names Ash told me she wanted to name her kids. Leah. Odessa. Ezra.

Isabelle.

Asmodeus laughed. It echoed as if coming out of a deep abyss. I needed to buy time with banter but I was shell-shocked. I wanted a confrontation but every valiant accusation fell flat. There was nothing left to say.

"I loved you."

"I do love you, you know. I don't think you get that part. It doesn't fit in with your worldview, your little dream of a white picket fence. I'm sorry I don't have the right status or money or respectability, but I am giving you *something*. Power."

"You don't even believe that, do you?" I said.

I recalled the image of Izzie impaled on a spike. When a toy was no longer fun it was thrown out.

"Fuck you. I don't love you," I spit. Something crossed Ash's face that I couldn't place. "This isn't sustainable. You're going to run out of girls. You already have."

"Every utopia is built on something. Remember that."

The swirling wickedness overhead began to collapse onto us, casting dirt and ice across the chapel until what was left of the walls fell with a thud. A giant shadow gasped in the middle of the great wind. Legion's corporeal form was made up of many strange creatures, ones with claws and piglet faces. Serpents and eyes and locusts descending from above. A bestiary of all that came before plummeting down on the just and the wicked alike. The floor was coated with sludge that bubbled and dripped down from the heaving mass, and slowly, piece by piece, Legion's many-faced body descended. King of Hell, Lord of Wrath. I saw his true face among the malevolent noise.

My conversion therapist.

He looked just like before. Smiling, laughing. A sudden nauseating smell overpowered my senses as the world around me went black.

When I woke I couldn't tell how much time had passed. I was somewhere dark. Low voices gurgled a stream of incoherent words and sounds. "Gehenna," they said. Strange long creatures writhed along the ground. In the darkness it was difficult to make out how many of them were there. Worse than LSD. Somewhere in the distance a hot column blazed. Ladders sprouted from the ground, seemingly going nowhere into the inky eternal night. The ground was covered with ruby-red coals, shifting beneath me like sand, but when I examined the individual grains I realized that they were in fact millions of tiny eyes wide with terror and mouths screaming in unison. A hulking lizard with two bony wings rattled through the air. I was in a ditch of some kind. This wasn't the world I wanted to inherit.

Hell. Legion had taken me somewhere he could be sure I would stay frozen in terror. I didn't think I was dead. I could still feel my body. Perhaps Legion was going to trade places with me. He would take over my body and toss me into the pits of Tartarus. The demonic monstrosity of trans girls explained. Hieronymus Bosch had gotten the underworld's geography right. The eyes, the strange creatures thronging the air. Ezekiel's angels seemed a delight compared to the silent beings around me. Recalling the experience now feels like trying to retell an acid dream, something so revelatory that flattens in the rearview mirror.

Flames burst in the distance. Far enough away to mark me safe but close enough to be disquieting. Loneliness gnawed at my body like the stench of summer, like sinking into a depression bed and noticing that the water glass was just out of reach. Like being dumped. Like being raped and having your friend say it wasn't rape. Like splitting out of your body and finding you are tied to the moment: crucified in the selfish destructive numbing fire. The moment before self-harm. When every window feels shut. Every escape route closed off. No one loves you. In fact, no one likes you. You are the shit of the earth. God loves everyone except you. You deserve the life you had and the one to come, never-ending tribulation without deliverance. You are not a woman. You are an abomination. Your mother thinks so. Your father left you. Your friends can barely tolerate your feeble mind. You are not special or interesting even in your pain. Plenty of others have gone through the same thing, but better. My mind shut off. When I opened my eyes again, I saw Ash moving in and out of a skeletal garden.

"I can say I loved you if that makes you feel better . . ." she said.

Somewhere in the distant ruins, Dagon was crawling over a mountain of sand. A giant hound that I recognized instinctively as the witch Hecate darted past. In the distance, I saw the Lords of Gluttony, Sloth, and Greed. They whirled around, closing in on me. Ash changed form once more, revealing my grandmother.

"Come with my, my child . . . Come with me into the depths!"

I couldn't take it. The wounds stung as if made fresh again, oozing all over my body. I tried to close my eyes against the ones I loved turned into diabolical freaks. Slurs clogged the air. *Bitchwhoresluttrannycuntfuckupasshole.*

YOU STUPID GIRL.

EVIL GIRL.

YOU VILE BITCH.

YOU WILL DIE ALONE.

YOUR MOTHER DOES NOT LOVE YOU.

GOD DOES NOT LOVE YOU.

HE WILL NOT SAVE YOU.

THE TRUTH WILL NOT SET YOU FREE.

EVERYONE WHO HAS EVER LOVED YOU HAS LEFT YOU.

GROTESQUE SHEMALE!

YOU WILL NEVER PASS.

HELL IS YOUR INHERITANCE.

YOU WILL NOT MAKE IT OUT ALIVE.

You lonely, lonely cunt.

The ghosts of my past were losing their shape, fumbling with exposed skeletons. Maggots crept up from the ground. I wanted to bury myself in the holes they'd dug. I didn't have the strength to deal. Fighting the horror felt pointless. Even raising my hand felt like an accomplishment in the thick of the noxious smell of death. Loose tongues scattered across the ground, slimy eyeballs in a wicked dance. Blood sprung up from the ground like a geyser, thick red juice filling the air. Someone was laughing.

My conversion therapist stepped out from behind an onyx wall. Wearing a wide grin and his one earring. His body was different, and I couldn't place how at first. Then I noticed his heart, beating outside his chest and wrapped tightly by two snakes. He was wearing gloves and holding a rusty shovel dripping with red. He licked the shovel and let the blood run to the back of his throat.

"Like honey," he said.

"Is it really you?"

"Why split hairs?"

"For naming purposes."

"Do you think, little bitch, you can contain me with a name? This isn't that kind of fairy tale. There is no trick to stop the Great Deceiver."

"Should I use the name I know?"

"Call me Israfel. Call me Legion. Call me whatever you'd like." He looked at my arms. They'd gotten all sliced up. "Death is here."

Death really was a proud asshole, chilly and armed with his Cerberus, all Greek and hollow with snakes for teeth. He stood above the pit looking down at Legion and me. His eyes were obscured by thick sunglasses. I twinged. He was not as scary as Legion but something about him left me feeling exhausted. Empty.

"He's ready for you," Legion said. "Death will hand you to the devil."

Legion crawled on all fours to close the few feet between us. He stood up and bit my neck. Raw, fleshy, pink, red. Green ghosts flew overhead. As the cloud of contemptuous witnesses gathered, I heard the squeals of a hundred piglets. There really was only one way out. Tethering wasn't the easy process everyone had made it seem like. Legion stayed close, getting ready to claim me. Blood dripped down my neck. It smelled like piss.

"Call me Marah, for the Almighty hath dealt bitterly with me," I said at last. The Book of Ruth had always served me when it came to dealing with men. I spit on the ground. "I won't repent."

Something hot licked my field of vision, diminishing the flames into a pinprick of light. I blacked out.

The sound of police sirens woke me.

Hazel ran up to me, I couldn't tell from where. She was losing it. I looked at the sallow color of her skin in the firelight. The pillar of smoke must've finally attracted outside attention. A fire truck pulled up behind the state troopers.

"Are you okay?" she asked. I could barely form words. My body was caked in mud and soot. "You were in there forever. I'm so glad you're okay. I helped Indigo, Esther, and Elle get away. I haven't seen anyone else though."

I looked at her without registering anything she said. I couldn't shake the vision of Legion in the shape of my conversion therapist, though the nightmare was supposed to be over. I couldn't feel any part of my body. *Eloi, Eloi, lama sabachthani?* What is a girl worth to the Almighty?

The men around me screamed at us to get on the ground. I closed my eyes and burrowed my head into Hazel's arms as she held my limp body like a pietà.

MOTHER KNOWS BEST

My mom poured two cups of tea. It was the cheap black kind she bought in bulk at the grocery store. She took hers with milk and sugar, I liked honey. She always loved English Breakfast but usually got decaf so she could drink it all day and night. I inherited my caffeine dependence from her. When I was seventeen, I made her get a coffee machine a few days after she quit cold turkey.

"You finally came to see me," she said. I could smell old hard-boiled eggs whenever she opened the trash can to throw something else away. "I was thinking about your grandma recently. She hated boiled eggs. Can you believe that?"

On the way over Hazel had tried to dissuade me from seeing her. She said the last thing I needed was more trauma. But there we were, surrounded by lacy wall hangings and dusty mahogany furniture. The Doberman was yelping next door, even louder than I remembered. Hazel was scrutinizing the tchotchkes. The stairs were littered with bath products that I assumed were meant to make it upstairs at some point. The

TV was silently playing *Dateline*. I caught a few muffled words about body parts and trash bags.

"I hate that stuff," my mom said and swiftly turned the channel. On-screen, petite blond woman with perky tits made an egg white omelet in a pink kitchen. My mom's kitchen was periwinkle. She painted it herself a few years after I went to college.

"How have you been?" she asked, handing me a mug with Garfield on it. I knew she was about to serve us some strangely assembled lunch. Then, before I could answer, she continued, "You look a little beat-up."

"I've been okay," I said. My injuries weren't as severe as Esther's or Elle's, but I'd seen better days.

"So you two were at a little camp?" she prodded, eyeing me as if to assess the truth of my answers.

"Kind of," I said.

"Your voicemails were so cryptic. And then they just stopped coming."

"My phone broke."

"Well then." She laughed. "Is this Ash?"

Hazel frowned.

"I'm Hazel," she said. "I'm surprised she's never mentioned me."

"My daughter has a way about her," my mom said. I wasn't sure what "way" she was referencing, but it didn't sound like a compliment. "Are you going back to New York soon?"

The early-afternoon light drifted in from the glass sliding door that led to the small backyard. My mom was proud of her porch. In the spring she planted sunflowers. They used to be taller than me. Beyond the yard there was a small wood. I used to go on long walks through the birch trees. And when I started smoking pot, I'd hide out there wearing the leather jacket my dad had left behind.

"Yes," I said. Hazel raised an eyebrow at me, then relaxed into the paisley couch, scrolling quietly.

"You look so . . . weighed down," my mom said.

"I haven't gained weight," I said.

"That's not what I mean."

"I meant that you look older," she went on, "experienced or something."

"Thanks," I said.

"I wish I could've been there for you more these past few years."

Hazel looked up, suddenly interested. I glared at her to stay out of it.

"I'm going to go to the bathroom," she said and got up, fumbling around the suburban maze of the first floor.

"What do you mean?" I asked, returning to the smoke bomb my mom had lobbed into our living room.

"You know," my mom said and gestured emptily. There was no end to what she could've been gesturing at. The clock. The bed for the cat that died years ago. The coffee table littered with cooking magazines and coupons.

The TV flickered. A commercial featuring the Famous Trans-Girl Actress holding a Gucci bag while caressing a black horse played. That was the life Hazel wanted. Maybe she would get it. I expected my mom to make some comment, but she said nothing. She probably didn't even know who the girl was.

"I wish I'd known what to do . . ."

We sat in silence. I thought I could hear Hazel peeing from

two rooms over. Strange to have another trans person in my childhood home. It felt less like a menacing fun house and more like a small golden cage.

"Thank you," I said, cutting her off and rocking uneasily on the couch.

The house was still except for the vents cracking with the shifting air pressure. Maybe it was the heating. I wasn't sure I wanted to dig into the cavern of truth, unearthing pain that I'd barely touched with her before. My mom did not try to say whatever it was that she wanted to say again. We let it lie. Hazel reemerged a few minutes later and sat down next to me. I watched her scroll through Greyhound options.

"Can you drive us to the station after I find a ticket?" she asked.

"Of course," my mom said. I couldn't figure out the look on her face. She made me feel like a child again, how I tried to foretell every possible emotional response. I blinked a few times, the debris of hell still on me.

"I'll be right back," I said.

The stairs were just as creaky as they were when I was a kid. Framed photographs hung on every wall. There were a few of us at church picnics, one of me and my dad before he left, another of me riding a bike for the first time. There weren't any from high school or college. No one cares after a certain age. Even though I have a gasoline-soaked nostalgia for those times, my mom clearly didn't. Maybe parents just like the innocent times better. But I remember. Childhood wasn't so nice either. Once, a neighborhood kid threw a frog at a tree so hard its guts littered the forest floor. I wanted to tell on him, but I didn't.

Now I can't remember whether or not he made me throw a frog too.

My room was empty except for a bed with lilac sheets, a large mirror, and my grandma's ashes. They were partly why I wanted to come back. After the shock of seeing my grandma as a demon I wanted to make sure that her remains were safe. I opened the urn and saw the gray powder. None of us knew why she'd asked to be cremated. She was the first in the family to request it. I wished I could've visited her grave, it would've been more romantic.

A few of the King Arthur books my grandma gave me were stacked in the closet. I grabbed one and held it to my chest. I stood by the window that opened onto an elm tree in the front yard. We lived at the end of a small cul-de-sac. Everyone else had moved away: the other single mom, the family even more religious than mine, the couple with the rosebushes. But not the Doberman. He would be there forever. That dog was vicious. I closed the window. The vent bellowed.

During my childhood, every time I returned home from a conversion therapy session, I dropped my backpack on my bed and went outside for a walk. The whole house felt stagnant, like no amount of energy could move anything inside it. It was the house. If I only knew what I wanted, I could leave and try to get it. But I didn't know anymore. I didn't know if there was anything to want that wasn't so tied to the trauma. I still didn't want to be one of the Hot Freelance Girls. I just wanted what little power they had, localized as it was. I thought they had a purpose. I thought they shimmered in their slip dresses and dangly silver earrings, unlike me and my combat boots. I kept thinking I could write my way into freedom but all I did was write about my little walks. It wasn't freeing. It was depressing.

I couldn't just write a full account of my life in search of what had gone wrong. All I had were pictures of femme freaks on motorcycles, posts about the monstrosity of desire, abolition articles that offered noncarceral solutions, Prada archives featuring Uma Thurman looking like a princess, poems, comics about prune Danishes, videos of women using rainbow sponges as stamps, pigs kissing, Ursula K. Le Guin short stories. They meant a lot to me and nothing to anyone else.

I felt the shadow of something sinister in my room as the smell of sulfur filled it. Not today. I would not entertain any goats asking me about pleasure or disembodied pigs who spoke in tongues. I turned my back on the shadow. There would be no final confrontation. I decided to give myself the day off.

"I found tickets, babe," Hazel yelled from the bottom of the stairs.

"Can we get a muffin on the way?" I shouted back.

PIETÀ

We sat in the Coney Island diner, debating what to order and sipping burnt coffee. It was raining, the kind of interminable storm that no one wants to wade into. Hazel and I had just gotten back into the city a few hours ago. My ass was sore from the bus ride.

"Well," I said suggestively.

Hazel stirred another Sweet'N Low into her coffee and blew on the steam.

"I'm sorry," Xiomara said. "We missed you. We're glad you're back."

The diner was playing an old Hank Williams song. There was only one waitress working, walking around wearing the grim look of duty.

"I wanted to go to water parks. I wanted fireworks. I wanted the whole world," I replied.

Ash and I had always talked about going everywhere. When I was taking care of her after her surgery, I would make a pot of tea and we would sit on her porch in the cool California morning sun. Pale-blue light stroking lemon trees, bushes, and sand. There was a carnal joy to inanimate objects, like they meant something. Before her I didn't understand love. I did not understand words in the contexts they were usually placed in.

"We never got to see Coney Island together." I sighed.

"We're here now," Xiomara said.

Somewhere in the wet darkness, the sun was dripping. I still didn't know what love was. That was the worst part. Only having felt a part of it, like one line in a Cy Twombly painting. One bit of something wild and erasing. Was there anything as holy as her face in the morning? Even after everything went down at the commune, even after I knew I'd been betrayed, I wasn't sure. I was already romanticizing.

Love has always been a structured politic for queer artists and hopefuls. Arthur Russell, Félix González-Torres, David Wojnarowicz, Derek Jarman. But the girls. The girls did not get their white lace tied together with a smile. Not Greer Lankton or Candy Darling. Not even cis queen Joni Mitchell found a lasting love to buy her a dishwasher and a coffee percolator. She bought them herself. Love is a monument to the body, acting out of idolatry toward other bodies. I know I have been taught that both idolatry and the body are bad, but my body is an idol worth wrecking my body for and my body wanted her body.

Xiomara squelched ketchup splotches all over her plate. Hazel was still pissed. She was frustrated there was no reasonable way to explain the demonic to them. I told her on the bus that no one would believe us. She only believed herself because she'd seen it. Nora kept looking at Hazel like she was a ghost, and she was. There wasn't much left for either of us to say about the karmic flip we'd endured.

“I need a cigarette,” Hazel said.

“Me too,” Nora said, squeezing my hand as she exited the booth.

“It’s raining,” Xiomara yelled after them as they walked under the fluorescents.

“Hazel needs a second.”

“They’ll get soaked,” Xiomara said.

“They’ll be okay. I think Nora’s gonna try to figure things out with Hazel.”

“You think?”

“Yeah. She thinks they’re meant to be. She told me before I left town. Now that Hazel’s left and come back she probably thinks it’s time.”

“Good luck to them,” Xiomara said.

“Did anything interesting happen while I was gone?”

“No, not really. With you and Hazel gone I just led a normal, happy life. No bullshit.”

“Come on,” I said.

“I worked. Fucked a few girls. Nothing serious. I’m a homebody now.”

“That sounds nice.”

Her voice was distant. I wasn’t sure how I fit in her life anymore. I used to be the one who kept all of us together. Not because of my charming personality but because I was the one who kept the group chat active. Hazel and I hadn’t talked about it too much on the bus, but I was pretty sure that she was going to try to get back to L.A. Hazel thought being free was important. I was less decided on the point. That scared her, I think. She did not like to be tied down.

“Are you really okay?”

"I don't know," I said.

"Did you really want to come back to New York? Or did Hazel just strong-arm you into it?"

"Where else would I go, Xiomara? Portland? L.A.? Chicago?"

"Somewhere less expensive. Minneapolis."

"What would I do there? I'd have to wait months to get hormones from some underfunded Planned Parenthood."

"Don't act like you don't have options. We can help," she said. I knew she wasn't saying it to make me feel like a burden, but I clawed my coffee tighter anyway.

"I just need to find a job. Something better. A cheaper apartment. Maybe a nondemonic therapist."

"That sounds good," Xiomara said. She looked at me for a minute and then took a long sip of her coffee.

Hazel and Nora came back in. They sat closer together than before, but I couldn't tell how much to read into it.

"Can we get more coffee?" Xiomara asked as the flinty waitress walked by.

We sat across from one another drinking coffee until work called. Xiomara went to the library, Hazel to an audition for a commercial we all knew she wouldn't get, and Nora without saying anything about her next destination.

Indigo tried to call me as I was running down the boardwalk trying to escape the thick sheet cake rain. I let my phone go to voicemail, but after a few minutes of waiting under an entryway, nothing appeared. Okay. Onward. There wasn't much she or I could've said to each other. I was over trying to build something on top of trauma. No one had heard from Ash since the incident. Indigo, Esther, and Elle looked around in the woods for a few more hours but found no one. After a while they bailed, not wanting to miss their own chance at escape. I don't blame them.

I still missed her sometimes. I hated her sometimes too. On our drive back through the heartland I had written a postcard to her. But there was nowhere to send it.

I want you to tell me you love me, not because of my gender or out of my gender, I want you to tell me, not with your words, I want you to tell me you love me with your body, so my body does not feel like loss.

My day was a vacuum. At some point I had to make it back to Xiomara's apartment for the night. I would have to apply to a million jobs and not just let momentum carry me wherever it wanted, but actually shape things myself. Write a living will. Forge something. Testify. Feeling was spreading back into my extremities. Jesus hung somewhere far away from me in a bloody cocoon.

The aquarium looked like a giant white tent surrounded by blue Jenga blocks as I approached it. By the time I made the conscious choice to head inside, I was in a daze. I bought my ticket from a tired-looking woman who was talking to her coworker about the best bodega in the area. She liked the one that always had Diet Dr Pepper.

I started wandering through the exhibits without looking at a map. Water always called me. I walked past a tiny coral reef fluttering with seahorses. The dolphins slept quietly, low and wondrous. I passed a tank filled with blushing electric jellyfish, spreading like targets. Halfway down the hallway, I heard the squall of penguins ahead. I wandered away from the arctic corner and found myself thronged on both sides by stingrays in little salty pools. A young woman carrying a bucket of tiny fish sped past me. None of the signs around me suggested that I pet the rays, but they didn't discourage it either.

In my head I imagined coming face-to-face with a transformative whale, but ahead there was just a long tunnel of grinning sharks. The lights flickered. Part of me wanted to turn back. It'd be the perfect demon trap. But when I reached the tunnel, there was only silence. My body hummed. I had no interior monologue. The cerulean tanks sparkled with rays of artificial light. I wanted to be happy. For a few minutes I did not picture Ash's or my conversion therapist's faces. I only saw the seaweed floating in the water.

Toward the end of the tunnel, I made eye contact with a nurse shark. She didn't move or anything, just stared straight at me. I stood looking at her for a while. This was it, I thought. Freedom. Not freedom from or freedom to, just freedom. I felt light, like my whole body was floating with the sharks. Selah.

ACKNOWLEDGMENTS

Dana, without knowing what love is, I don't think I could write about what it isn't so clearly. You made this book possible. From bouncing around ideas to introducing me to the joy of horror movies, I'm so grateful to you for coming into my life and teaching me about pleasure. You are such a kind, thoughtful, intelligent partner. Thank you for making me laugh and walking this path alongside me.

Alf, for always sitting with me on park benches these past few years, making sure I ate, encouraging me go outside of the house even when I was incredibly depressed, and believing in me. The hype man we all deserve. The friend we cherish. This book wouldn't exist without your tenacity and kindness.

Joselia, I treasure all the times we've talked on the phone for hours and hours. We still do that sometimes. We talked about cutting ties, exes, candle magic, codependency, writing, disability, gender, community, and love. Always love. You helped me realize I am a writer and that is no small gift. One day we will sit across from each other in conversation at the New York Public Library. It is a gift to be in conversation with you and to be your friend.

Thank you to my agent, Julia Masnik, for believing in such a strange book and reminding me of my ability to accomplish something so Herculean. I couldn't have done this without you and the kindness you brought to this book even when I nursed doubt. To Sareena Kamath for taking a chance on this book and enthusiastically supporting great genre work and understanding the kind of horror I was writing so intimately and offering such genuine, sharp edits. Thank you to the entire Saga team, including Camryn, Ella, Evangeline, Jéla, Joe, Karintha, Savannah, and Tim.

Frankie for being in the trenches of sisterhood with me. Stella for being excited when I couldn't. My mother, Kate Bornstein, for telling me life doesn't have to be profound and taking me to Tiffany and Co. Cecilia Gentili for calling my breasts *Playboy* level. We miss you. Rachika Nayar for getting me into trans women on motorcycles, E Taylor for letting my write criticism and supporting my career when I was just starting, Russell Sheaffer for your truly proud queer parenthood, my uncle Jon for getting me into King Arthur, Casey Gregonen for being by my side always even after a decade. Leah Abrams, Heather Akumiah, Karen Yuan, and Maria Xia for being there for my writing and cheerleading me on and always having me be one of the girls. My family—Jenna and Charlie and my parents. The outlets and editors that published my early fiction: Rachelle Toarmino at Peach, Maddie Crum and Michelle Lyn King at *Joyland*, Alexandra Tanner at Triangle House, Paul Thompson at the *Los Angeles Review of Books*, Miriam Gordis and Ella Fox-Martens at *Angel Food*. Thank you to Bud Smith, Harron Walker, Meg, Zachary Lynn, Sarah Thankam Mathews, Agnes Walden, Gretchen Felker-Martin, Tony Tulathimutte, CRIT, Rax Will, Anais, Mary South, Kelly Link, for your thoughts on my fiction and writing and cheerleading to push through.

ABOUT THE AUTHOR

Grace Byron is a writer from the Midwest based in Queens. Her writing has appeared in *The New Yorker*, *New York* Magazine, *The Nation*, *Bookforum*, *Frieze*, the *Los Angeles Review of Books*, and *The Baffler*, among other outlets. Find her @emotrophywife.